WHELPS

EARTH DRAGONS BOOK 3

CHARLENE HARTNADY

DEDICATION

To my slightly nutty and yet very proper Nonna, thank you for instilling the love for books and reading firmly inside me.

You are, in truth, unlike most grandmothers. No sweet treats, or presents, in fact, no spoiling whatsoever, and yet, I wouldn't trade you for the world. You gave us time and affection instead. Things money could never buy. Love you always!!

CHAPTER 1

Georgia looked down at her finger. *What?* She checked her other hand. *Nope!* Her papercut from that morning was gone. How was that possible? She obviously hadn't cut herself as badly as she thought. Then again, it was just a papercut. Sore but hardly deep or deadly. No wonder it was gone. Without a trace though? She realized she was still looking at her fingertips when Ian Joyce spoke to her.

"What about the father?" He leaned forward, folding his arms on the table. He looked the picture of calm. The tight lines around his mouth told a different story. "You mentioned that he isn't aware of the situation." His eyes narrowed slightly as he scrutinized her.

Georgia worked hard at sitting still. She shook her head slowly. "You don't have to worry about him, he's not in the picture. It was one night…" She felt her cheeks heat, the need to squirm in her chair increased. "A mistake."

Oh boy, was it ever. That night was the mother of mistakes!

"Yes, but he's bound to find out about this…" He glanced down at her distended belly. "It's hard to miss that you're pregnant." He smiled in a way that was kind and understanding. The lines around his mouth didn't soften, however. "You *have* told him, haven't you?"

"We're worried we will get our hopes up only to have them… dashed." Christine Joyce smiled as well; her smile was sad. "It's happened before." She looked at her husband who gripped her hand tightly in his.

"The father isn't from Dalton Springs. He was here for one night." She shrugged. "I only know his first name. He was supposed to be in town for a convention for martial arts or something." She frowned. "I've tried to find him based on that, and his first name, but no luck. I tried at the hotel he was staying at, but I couldn't remember the room number. The hotel wasn't forthcoming about previous guests anyway." She pushed out a breath. "He's long gone. It's not like Dalton Springs is much of a tourist destination. I doubt very much that he's ever coming back here. Even if he did, I doubt he would want anything to…" she cleared her throat, trying to tamp down on her emotions, "do with this baby. He told me he didn't want kids." She put a hand to her belly, feeling the baby move inside her. It only made her feel worse. Feeling the life inside her. Growing every day. A part of her. A part she was having to deny. She couldn't grow too attached. Couldn't afford to, for her own sanity.

Georgia removed her hand, placing it on her lap instead. She ignored the little kicks in her womb and focused on the couple in front of her. The couple who wanted to adopt this baby. They would be perfect parents.

They seemed like good people. They had money. Christine was leaving her job as an accountant to focus on being a mom full time. She'd make the best mom. The kind who went for walks with the baby in the stroller. The kind who took their kid to the park. Who walked them to school and back every day. The kind who helped with homework and baked cookies. They would be able to offer this child everything she couldn't. Everything and more. The kid would have both parents and a loving home with means.

"Okay." Ian Joyce nodded, some of those lines disappearing. "So, the father is most likely never going to be an issue. What about you Miss Hewlett? You might change your mind."

Mrs. Joyce sniffed. "Please don't misunderstand, we are desperate for a child. We want you to pick us. We don't want to sound like we're being difficult, but," she swallowed, "it's happened before. After the birth. As soon as the mother held the baby, she decided she wanted to keep her."

I want this baby.

I want to keep this—"That's not going to happen." Her voice was firm. Georgia sat up straighter in her chair. "I can't be a mother to this child."

Christine Joyce leaned forward. "How can you be so sure? It might all change when you hold him or her in your arms."

"I'm very sure. It can't happen." She shook her head vehemently. "You see, I have no other choice but to give this baby up. None!" She shook her head again.

"There's always a choice, Miss Hewlett," Ian said. His hair had the beginnings of grey at his temples. His eyes were crinkled around the edges. She could see desperation in their depths.

"I work two jobs to make ends meet." She looked from Ian to Christine and back again. "I have no support." Her voice cracked as she said the last. "I'm sorry." She cleared her throat. "I can't afford to take any time off work. I can't afford daycare." She shrugged. "My baby would be better off," she rubbed her lips together, "in a loving home with two parents who can look after him or her. That's the bottom line. Short of some kind of miracle, I literally can't keep this child." She swallowed thickly. "I'm doing what's best for my baby."

"That's commendable." Mr. Joyce's eyes looked solemn. She couldn't help but notice that some of the tension had left him. "You've asked for visitation?" He raised his brows and looked at his wife, who widened her eyes. "Truth is… we're not sure how comfortable we are with that setup. It might be confusing for the child."

"We wouldn't have to tell the child about me being their biological mother until they were old enough to understand, but yes, it's important to me that I am a part of this kid's life. I can't afford to keep this baby but that doesn't mean I want to cut all ties either. I can't be a mother to my child, but I can be there."

"Thing is," Christine said, "we want to start our lives as a family without interruption or… It's a strange request, that's all. It would leave things open for you to—"

"This baby would be legally yours. You would have all the say. The two of you would be the parents." It hurt her to even say the words, but she forced them out. It was how it had to be. "I would be a friend of the family or something. We can figure it out. I won't be at your house every day or anything. Maybe bi-weekly." She shrugged.

Mr. Joyce shook his head. "It might be more difficult for you if you see the baby regularly versus cutting ties. Have you thought of that?"

"All I do is think about it. I don't care about myself… I'm not important. It's my baby who is most important. I think this child would ultimately want to know that they were loved… in the long run, that is. That I made an effort. That I didn't just abandon him or her." Her eyes welled but she blinked back the tears.

"I can't help but think that it would be a confusing arrangement. I'm just not sure it would work for us…" He looked like his mind was working a mile a minute.

"I'm afraid I have to insist." Georgia pressed her lips together for a moment. "There are other couples interested."

"Oh." Christine looked down, she clasped her hands together and squeezed.

Georgia really liked the Joyces, she hadn't planned on playing this card but what choice did she have? They needed to understand the bigger picture. They were good people. They ticked every box. They also lived fairly close by. Only thirty minutes' drive. All the other couples were far away. Not only that, the one couple didn't look all that happy together. They pretended to be. Tried really hard, but the cracks were there. The other couple was wealthy but too focused on their careers. The third couple was very young. They didn't feel right for this child. They'd also let slip that they were hoping for a girl. Georgia had no idea what the sex of this baby was. "I'm going to be honest," Georgia said. "I'm leaning towards the two of you for the adoption."

Christine smiled brightly and clutched her chest.

"Really?" she gushed. "You had me worried there for a moment."

"Yes, really, but I have to be a part of this child's life. I won't interfere. He or she will be yours. I have made peace with that." Her chest clenched tight. "It will be more difficult for me this way. To watch him or her grow up. To hear them call you mom." The clenching tightened. "It will be almost unbearable, but it is something I will endure. I have to give my child away. There is no other option for me, but I refuse to abandon this baby. I hope you understand that."

"Okay." Ian nodded. "We will need to discuss it, but it is more understandable now that you have explained." He smiled at his wife who beamed back.

"I agree, it makes more sense now." Christine turned to her, still beaming.

"Let us know when you're ready and we can take care of the paperwork."

"Okay." She nodded. Sooner rather than later would be better.

"The lady from the agency said you are around six months along. I know it's not an exact science but what is the due date?"

"By my calculations, it should be early June."

Christine frowned. "Your calculations? You *have* been to see a doctor?"

Georgia felt her cheeks heat all over again. "I'm afraid not. I haven't been able to afford it."

Mr. Joyce frowned deeply. "Why? Have you applied for Medicaid or…?"

"I can't," she shook her head. "I earn above the minimum threshold."

"But then surely—"

"My mother is ill. She has Alzheimer's." Georgia pressed her lips together.

"Oh." Christine covered her mouth. "That's terrible."

"Yes," Georgia paused. "It's been three years since she was diagnosed. It's very rare if she even remembers who I am anymore. Although, she still has the occasional good day."

"Must be tough." Mr. Joyce looked uncomfortable. He shifted in his chair.

"She's in a home and needs full-time care. Thankfully, she is on an insurance plan, but it doesn't cover all her needs. Not even close. I am all she has. I'm responsible for her wellbeing. Every spare cent goes to her needs. I make do. I live on very little but the debt is slowly mounting. I can't work any more than I do now."

"Such a burden on you," Mr. Joyce interjected, shaking his head.

"I don't see it that way."

His eyes widened. "I didn't mean it like that. I—"

"I know you didn't." Georgia smiled, trying to diffuse the situation. "This has been really tough on me. My mother has to come first. I knew I was most likely pregnant but didn't take a test for weeks. In truth, I buried my head in the sand because I knew I would have to give this baby up. I've reached a point," she blinked back the tears, "where I can't do that anymore. I have to face reality. I have to do what's right for this baby." She was wrong not to have sought medical help. She was wrong to have waited this long. Facing up to reality had been an impossibility for her. "Going for an ultrasound would've cost a whole week's worth of food. I quite literally had to choose between eating or going for a check-up. It's no excuse, of course." Guilt rolled around inside her. She lived with it.

"You really don't have to explain, Miss Hewlett. Give it some real thought. When you are really ready, you give us the word," Mr. Joyce looked a little flustered, "and we'll help out." He shrugged. "You need medical care. You will need to see a doctor to ensure all is well… um… before we can proceed, but that's just a formality. You need vitamins and," he looked down at the dress she had squeezed herself into, "maternity wear… healthy food. We're here for you now, Miss Hewlett."

She nodded. Her first instinct was to turn him down. "Okay… thank you." She nodded again. She couldn't say no. She had to accept the help, for the baby.

"Just give us the go-ahead and we'll arrange everything," Christine added, with a smile. "You're not alone anymore."

Funny, she still felt alone. Very alone. Then the baby kicked, and a tear trickled down her cheek. "Okay." She wiped her face. "That's great." She smiled.

CHAPTER 2

That evening…

G eorgia turned the corner, heading for the east wing. She waved at the approaching nurse. "Hello," she called out.

"Your mom isn't having a great day, I'm afraid." Nurse Tanya frowned, pushing her hands into her pockets.

"Okay." Georgia acknowledged. "Thanks for the heads-up."

"I know it isn't always possible, but mornings are better. She tends to go downhill as the day goes by."

"I know." Pity she had to work most mornings. She was an admin clerk at a marketing agency. She'd had to meet the Joyces during her lunch break.

The other woman gave her a pat on the arm as she walked past. "You're a good daughter," she said. "Your mother is lucky to have you."

Georgia smiled and nodded once. She didn't always feel like a good daughter. There were days when she wanted to leave and never come back. She always would though.

Georgia sucked in a deep breath as she arrived at her mom's door. She turned the knob and went in. "Hi, mum!" She closed the door behind her on a soft click.

Her mom looked her way. There was zero recognition in her eyes. "I don't want any tea," she announced, looking back at the television, which was on but set to mute. Loud noises tended to aggravate her. Closed spaces aggravated her sometimes as well. She liked to watch the television. Usually. Sometimes even that was too much.

"I don't have any tea," Georgia said as she approached her mom's bed.

"I don't want lunch!" her mom yelled. "No lunch!" she shouted, shaking her head. Her hair was mussed.

"Okay, mom… that's okay. You don't have to have lunch." She shook her head slowly.

"No lunch!" Her mom's eyes widened. "Stop calling me that." Her voice had taken on a desperate edge. She sounded upset and confused. "Who are you? I don't want lunch. You shouldn't call me that."

"I'm here to clean your room." It was definitely one of those days. Georgia walked over to the closet and took out a broom. "Just to clean." She held up the cleaning equipment. Georgia began to sweep. She risked a quick glance at her mom, out of the corner of her eye.

She had, thankfully, calmed down and was quietly watching the television. Some days were like this. The bad days. The terrible days were worse. At least there was still the odd good day. Georgia lived for those days.

She swept the floor twice before putting the broom

away and sitting down next to her mom who completely ignored her. Georgia was content to sit there. It was one of those nature programs, something about penguins. Her eyes began to feel heavy.

As much as she wanted to, she couldn't give in to it. Three orders for cover designs had come in that day. She needed to get cracking when she got home. Two of the covers were customs. Only the one was a pre-made.

Her second job was designing e-book covers for the romance indie writers' community. Hours of work for mediocre pay, but hey, she wasn't complaining. It was a job. It was money. Not nearly enough, but money, nonetheless.

Georgia hoped to be able to go back to her position at the agency quite soon after the birth, considering her role wasn't physically taxing and also since she wasn't going to be raising the baby herself. No maternity leave required. Maybe a couple of days to get over the worst.

She couldn't afford any kind of time off, since it would be unpaid. She'd checked in with her boss, who hadn't been very helpful.

Slap! Pain exploded on the side of her face and she turned away to avoid being hit again. Georgia jumped to her feet, her face on fire.

Her mom was watching the television as if nothing had happened. "I told you," she rocked back and forth in her chair, "I don't want any supper." She rocked harder.

Georgia's cheek felt hot. It was probably red. Her skin stung. It didn't feel bad enough to form a bruise. She hoped not. Georgia had garnered more than her share of stares at work. Her boss had pulled her aside once to ask if everything was okay at home. She'd told him about her mother. That was the last time he had asked. It wasn't the end of the stares, however. Stares because she was bruised and battered at times. Stares because she was single and pregnant. She didn't relish the thought of the stares and the whispers after she gave this baby up. She grit her teeth for a few moments. It didn't matter. She'd get through it.

"It's okay, mom."

"Don't call me that. You aren't my Georgie. You aren't my…" Her eyes narrowed in confusion. "Who are you?" She was getting agitated. "Who…" Her brow was knitted together in confusion. Her eyes held fear.

"It's okay. You watch the penguins. I'm going to—"

"No pills!" her mom yelled. "Don't you dare try to make me take them." Her face was turning beet red.

"I'm leaving now." *Love you, mom,* she whispered in her mind. Her mother was in there somewhere. The woman who had tucked her in at night when she was a little girl. The woman who had read her bedtime stories. That's what made this so hard. It was like someone else was inhabiting her mother's body. She could be confused and frightened like a child one minute and downright dangerous the next, but she was still her mom.

Georgia closed the door to the room and put her hand to the wood.

"I know—"

Georgia jumped when she heard a voice behind her. "Oh, it's you, Jennifer."

"I didn't mean to give you a fright," the other woman said. She cradled a file in her arms.

"I know. I guess I'm a bit jumpy today." She forced her lips to form a smile.

"How are you feeling?" She glanced down at Georgia's

belly.

"I'm fine. A bit tired, but good."

"Your mom knows you come every day," Jennifer said. "She knows. She might not be able to acknowledge it, but deep down inside she knows it." The other woman patted her arm.

Georgia nodded. "I know, she told me the other day, when she was having one of her clear days. She cried about it. It's almost worse sometimes on her good days because she realizes how bad she is on all the other days."

"Hang in there." Jennifer touched the side of her arm. "You're doing all you can do – and then some."

Georgia nodded.

"Also," it looked bad, Jennifer's face turned grave, "they've upped your mom's meds. The tranquilizers that are helping keep her calm."

"One of the medications that aren't covered by her insurance?" Georgia groaned.

Jennifer nodded. "Yes, I'm afraid so."

Shit!! She was barely keeping up with the extras as it was. "Thanks for letting me know."

"So you don't get a fright when you see the bill at the end of the month. Also, she needs more shampoo, we're almost out."

Georgia nodded, feeling exhausted. She didn't have time to feel tired. There were those covers that needed designing. She also needed to rustle up some dinner. She put a hand to her belly. She needed to eat for the baby. "Thanks, Jen. I'll see you tomorrow."

"It's my day off tomorrow. You should try it, you know."

"What, taking a day off?"

Jennifer smiled. "Yes, you're going to burn out."

"Okay, I'll try it."

"Liar." Jennifer widened her eyes.

They both laughed, even though it wasn't really funny. Georgia said her goodbyes and headed home. It was already getting dark. She wished there were more hours in the day.

CHAPTER 3

S hale shifted, feeling his scales retract. Feeling his teeth turn blunt and his muscles tighten and shorten. The change felt good. It—

Next thing he was almost falling on his face when someone shoulder-knocked him, hard. He heard his brother's chuckle as he staggered to right himself.

"Sand. You dick!" Shale yelled, smiling all the while. "Then again," Shale snickered, "the only time you would stand even half a chance of taking me out is by blind-siding me."

"I wasn't trying to take you out, you little whelp! If I had been, you'd be down right now. I could take you any time. Anywhere!"

"Let's go, then." Shale opened his arms and broadened his stance. "Right here and right now, motherfucker."

"Nah!" Sand winked at him. "I'll let you off the hook today since you only just got back from the mines. You've had a busy day and it was a long flight here. It wouldn't be a fair fight."

"Who's the whelp now?" Shale snorted. "You're a scaredy-cat pussy."

"Talking about pussy," Sand changed the subject so quickly Shale almost got whiplash, "why have you been ignoring Topaz? I thought you and the female were tight. In fact, I thought you and she might—"

"What bullshit are you on about? I'm nowhere near ready to settle down and if I was… Topaz…" He shook his head. "We had some fun times together but… nope. Not happening!"

"No need to be so damned testy. I noticed your name down for this weekend."

Shale didn't feel quite as excited as he normally would at the prospect of the Stag Run. Although, if a certain fiery redhead were to pitch up, he might just—What the fuck was he saying? He didn't bed human females twice. It made them far too clingy. "Yep." He grinned. "I'm looking forward to it." *Big fucking time!*

"I was hoping you would give me your spot." His brother made a face. He knew he was trying his luck.

Shale snorted. "Not a chance! They're the best two weekends of the year. You can wait for your own turn."

"Four months is a long damn time to wait."

"If you like Topaz so much…"

Sand shook his head. "What, and take your sloppy seconds…?"

Shale had to laugh. "It wouldn't be the first time."

"I've matured since then."

"Like hell!" Shale laughed some more. "Life is too short for that kind of thinking. We need to get out there and have fun."

"Exactly! That's why I want you to give me your weekend."

"Not going to happen. There is a female in Dalton Springs who needs me this weekend. I don't know what she looks like. I don't know her name. All I know is that she desperately, desperately needs… this." He ran his hands down his body. "I'm not about to disappoint."

"Big-headed much?" Sand mock-frowned, his lips twitched with the start of a smile.

"Yes, actually." He palmed his cock. "Seems like I'm the twin who got lucky in every department."

"Like hell, asshole!" his brother choked out while laughing.

CHAPTER 4

Two days later...

*O**h my god!***
   This wasn't happening. It wasn't! This couldn't be happening. Georgia spotted Macy pacing back and forth on the pavement. Her friend walked up and then she walked back down. Macy looked to be in deep thought.

Making her realize that it was indeed happening. Macy's eyes widened as she spotted Georgia walking up. She stopped dead and then turned and walked towards her.

Okay! Calm down! Calm! She forced herself to suck in a deep breath. Maybe this was a sign. Maybe things would work out. Maybe—*No!* What the hell was she thinking? Nothing had changed. She needed to do the right thing and then she needed to follow through with her plan. Everything was decided. The Joyces were going to adopt this baby. She was going to the gynecologist on Tuesday for a scan. They were going to find out the sex of the baby. Make sure… *big gulp*… that everything was progressing normally. *Which it was!!* This was one of those run-of-the-mill pregnancies. Nothing to report. Nothing to see. It had to be. Why hadn't she just gone to the gynecologist before this? Her credit card was already shot to hell.

Stop!

The preliminary adoption paperwork was being drawn up. The final paperwork would be signed once her baby was born… once the Joyces' baby was born. It was all figured out.

Yeah, but—But nothing! She willed her stupid brain to shut up already.

"I'm so glad you picked up the phone. That you came so quickly. That you weren't—"

Despite the situation, she felt her lip twitch. "It's nine-thirty on a Saturday night. I was trying not to fall asleep in front of the television, trying to talk myself into going to bed. I have work in the morning. Several cover orders came in…" Georgia forced herself to stop talking and to stop fiddling with the edge of her shirt. "Have you been waiting long?"

Macy shook her head. "I literally just came outside. I kept my eyes on him to make sure he didn't leave."

"Are you sure it's him? Maybe you—"

"I'm very sure. Completely sure. Those guys were gorgeous… they… um… I wouldn't forget." She shook her head. "Their convention must be back in town, because they're all here. I recognize quite a few of them."

Georgia nodded. *Okay! She had this. It wasn't a big deal!*

Her friend's gaze softened. "Are you sure you want to do this? You don't have to, you know. That guy's a prick.

He's clearly here for one thing. Same as last time."

"I know exactly why he's here, he's trying to pick up a woman." *Trying… huh! Like hell.* Shale didn't have to try. He had women throwing themselves at him left right and center. No trying required. "And to answer your question, yes, I have to do this. I wish I didn't, but I have a conscience. I wouldn't be able to live with myself if I didn't inform him of the situation."

"I almost wish I hadn't spotted him," Macy grumbled. "I almost didn't call you."

Georgia smiled and squeezed her friend's arm. "But you couldn't not."

Macy rolled her eyes. "Something like that. Do you want me to go in with you?"

"Nope! This is something I have to tackle myself."

"Good luck! I'll be out here if you need me."

Georgia nodded. She took a deep breath and headed into the busy establishment. It took her all of five seconds to spot him. Just like before, their eyes locked instantly.

She was reminded of when they had met six months before and the cocky half-smile he threw her way as their eyes met.

Georgia smiled back. How could she not? She felt her cheeks heat and quickly looked away. She was there for a drink — maybe two — and then she was heading home. Besides, she didn't want to mooch off of Macy too much. Tomorrow was fast approaching. Day of rest… huh! Sunday was her busiest day of the week — at least it was for her sideline business. Her clients knew that. Orders would stream in on a Friday, all the way through Saturday. She had to be up early tomorrow morning. Not just that, she needed to be clear-eyed and clear-headed. She needed to deliver the goods. There were ten more designers like her online, all eager to fill the orders.

Since she didn't drink very often, more than two glasses of wine and she'd be hungover, and if she wasn't in bed by twelve, she'd turn into a pumpkin. Her body clock was well honed. There would be no sleep for her after six, it didn't matter what time of the morning she crawled into bed. Boom! Her eyes would open at six like clockwork. It had been like that for years.

There was no reason to stay longer anyway, since most guys were assholes. She'd learned that the hard way with Tate. No one would accept her situation. No one in their right mind anyway.

"Can I buy you a drink?"

She knew it was him without even turning his way. His voice was rich and deep. It had this smoky, sexy edge that suited him hands down.

Georgia turned her head, locking eyes with the most beautiful golden-colored irises. She'd never seen a shade quite like that before. Gorgeous eyes, framed by long, thick lashes. They were so unusual. Really gorgeous, like the rest of him. His hair was a sandy blond, it looked recently cut and was styled. His face was clean-shaven. He wore a lime green, button-down shirt that worked against the dark denim of his jeans. He filled his clothing out, that was for sure. Holy heck but he was gorgeous. Her danger alarm went off. This was a guy out for a good time. He needed to move right on.

Dimples appeared when he smiled again. Shit balls, despite the alarm bells, she was drooling and needed to stop right away. "Thanks, but I'm good." She held up her glass, trying to get rid of him. She wasn't there for that.

He leaned in, so close she could feel his heat. "You're really beautiful."

She looked at him skeptically. Her skin was too pale. Her hair too wild. Her freckles had freckles, for goodness sake. Not that there was anything wrong with her, but beautiful? Especially by this guy's standards. Please! She glanced around them, noticing how many beautiful women were in attendance. There were women with long lean limbs, many with high, perky boobs. Those with sleek blonde hair dos and beautifully tamed brunette heads.

"I can tell that you don't believe me." He took a sip of his beer, looking amused.

"I'm a ginger." She tugged on one of her spirals. Her hair was very long, at least, it was when it was wet. Her curls were so tightly spiraled that her hair only came to above her bra strap when it was dry. If she sneezed too hard it frizzed out, becoming big and uncontrollable.

"You have fiery, red hair. Very sexy." He gave her the once-over in a way that had her blood heating.

"Not everyone would find this wild mop sexy but," she laughed softly, "thank you... I guess." She took a sip of her own drink. "I need to find my friend." She looked around them.

"Why the rush?" He raised his brows.

She shrugged.

"You're all dressed up. Out for the night." He narrowed his eyes into hers. "You're single and yet... you don't want to talk to me." More raising of the brows. He cocked his head as well. Managing to look hot while doing it.

"Who says I'm single?" She folded her arms.

"Call it a hunch. I think you are. Very single — that is what makes me wonder... Either you're not attracted to me or," he licked his lips and of course, that too was sexy as hell, "you're scared." By his tone she knew which one he had in mind.

"I'm not scared," she mumbled, feeling her cheeks heat. Of course, by default, she'd just given away that she was, indeed, attracted to him. Why lie though? She might be attracted to the guy, but it didn't mean that she was going to do anything about it.

"I'm Shale." He held out his hand.

"And I need to find my friend." She glanced around them, *ignoring his hand, which he took back.*

"Who, the blonde with the long hair?"

She frowned. How did he know…?

Shale pointed to a couple locked in a hot and heavy kiss. "Is that her, by any chance?"

Oh wow! *"Um… yes."* It looked like Macy was getting all *kissy-face with one of the guys from his group.*

"Like I said before, I'm Shale. We're here on a martial arts convention."

"Martial arts?" Georgia was still watching Macy and Mr. *Muscles going at it. "I always thought martial arts fighters were leaner than you guys."* They were all so big and built. Every last one *of them.*

Shale grinned. "That's very observant of you. We're actually cage-fighters. Martial arts is a big part of the sport and… here we are."

"Where are you from then?"

"What does it matter?"

Oh! So, it was like that? Of course it was. She nodded, glancing at Macy. No! Hell no! *The guy had his hand on her ass… he was squeezing.* Go Macy! *Georgia had to bite back a grin.*

Her friend carried a few extra pounds and because of it, she lacked confidence, which was nuts since Macy was one of the most beautiful women she knew. Hands down. Yet, she'd been single for the longest time. Now look at her go. She noticed that both Macy's hands were on the guy's ass too.

"You look shocked," Shale said, right into her ear. Goosebumps rose up on her arms and down her back.

"It's just that Macy…" She shrugged. "She…" Wasn't *normally forward like that. "My friend isn't normally into this sort of thing."*

Now the couple was whispering to one another. There was plenty of giggling. Macy looked like a teenager. Her smile was wide. Her eyes glinted with mischief.

"What sort of thing would that be?" Shale asked, smiling. Those dimples did things to her.

"Well… you…"

Macy turned towards them, holding Mr. Muscles' hand, the big guy followed behind her. Macy widened her eyes at Georgia as they drew closer. She smiled and then made a face of disbelief. "Hi," Macy said as they arrived, "this is Rock."

"Rock?" What kind of name was that?

"It's my cage name." The big guy winked at her. He was cute, in a rough-around-the-edges kind of way.

Macy giggled and Rock threw an arm around her shoulders, drawing her into his side.

"My real name is Shaun, but my friends call me Rock." He held out his hand. Georgia took it. "I'm Georgia. It's good to meet you."

"Um…" Macy chewed on her lip, a smile toying with the edges of her mouth. "We're going to get out of here… if you don't mind, that is."

What?

Macy didn't do things like this.

"Can I have a quick word?" she whispered, leaning in towards Macy.

"Will you excuse me for a second?" she asked Rock or Shaun or whatever the hell the guy's name was.

"Of course." Mr. Muscles bent down and kissed her. He gripped her jaw softly in his huge hand, deepening the kiss for a second or two. Georgia glanced at Shale who, based on the grin he was sporting, clearly found the whole thing hilarious.

They moved to the side. "Who are you and what have you done with my friend?" Georgia asked as soon as they were far enough away.

Macy rolled her eyes. "You don't have to be so dramatic." She giggled. "I like him. I mean look at the guy, what's not to like?"

"You know this is just a... sex thing?"

Macy bobbed her brows. "I know exactly what it is. The guys are only here for one night and then they're headed back home to..." She frowned and then shrugged. "It just occurred to me that I have no idea where they are from. Not that it matters." She giggled again.

"Doesn't that worry you? That this is a one-night thing."

"Not at all." Macy shook her head.

"That's not like you."

"I'm living a little. I mean... look at him." She widened her eyes. "I'm just hoping he's big like that all over, and that he..." she bit down on her bottom lip for a second, "you know, is just as good at doing the deed as he is at kissing. It's been years since I last had sex. There might be cobwebs up there."

Georgia laughed and shook her head.

"Rock thinks I'm sexy. Just look at the women in this place — and he wants me..." she pointed at her chest. "I mean reeeeally wants me." She shrugged. "I'm hugely attracted to him as well, so, why the hell not?" She grinned. "They're staying at Dalton Spring Heights and are here for a convention."

"I know. His friend over there told me." Georgia glanced at Shale who was talking with Rock.

"Nothing bad will happen to me." Macy gripped her hand and squeezed. "If you don't want me to leave you, though, I'll turn him down and head home with you."

Georgia pushed out a breath. "I worry about you, that's all."

"I think I can handle it. I'm sure I'll be just fine."

"If you're sure, then I don't mind at all. I'll grab an Uber home."

She held up her half-finished wine. "As soon as I'm done with this."

"Wait a minute." Macy shook her head. "I said I'd pay for this whole evening. Drinks and the Uber. There and back. You can't afford it, Georgia."

Nope, she couldn't but she wasn't going to admit to it. "I'll be fine."

"No." Macy shook her head, digging in her bag. "Here," she held up a twenty, "that should cover the Uber and maybe even another glass of wine." Her friend grinned suddenly. "Although I'm pretty sure Handsome over there would be more than willing to spot you a drink."

"I'm not taking your money – and Handsome can kiss my ass."

"He sure looks like he wants to." They both broke out in peals of laughter. Macy quickly turned serious. "Please just take the money or I won't be able to go with Rock – and I realllllllly want to."

Georgia felt terrible. She felt useless. She felt helpless.

"Just take it, please," Macy pleaded.

"Okay," Georgia whispered. "Thank you!"

"Don't mention it. I dragged you out here." Then she smiled. "It needs to be said, Rock's friend is hot." Macy bobbed her brows. "He might even be more good-looking than Rock. Although I think Rock is so darned cute. But back to his buddy… wow! Handsome is a good nickname for him."

Georgia giggled. Where the hell had that come from? "That might be true but—"

"But nothing! It's been ages since you and Tate broke up. You should get back on the horse – and that guy's a freaking stallion."

Georgia choked out a laugh. "Easy, cowgirl. You head out with… Mr. Muscles over there. Don't worry about me." She held up the twenty.

"You really should go for it," Macy said in a singsong voice. "He wants you and he wants you bad. One night of fun!" Her friend turned serious. "You don't have any fun anymore. I understand why that is, but maybe you owe yourself this one time."

Georgia smiled. "I'll talk to him while I finish my drink." She shrugged. "You never know." She had no intention of going anywhere with Shale but if it helped Macy feel better about leaving, then she would say it anyway. She had a feeling that Mr. Muscles was going to be great for her friend's confidence.

"You mean that?"

"I swear it. I'll chat with Shale and if that leads somewhere, then so be it." Georgia did plan on finishing her drink. Why not? Then she'd head home and get some precious sleep. "You go and enjoy yourself," Georgia encouraged Macy, who beamed.

"You're sure?"

"I'm very sure." Georgia slapped Macy playfully on the arm. "Now you get out of here. Just be safe."

"Nothing is going to happen to me," she laughed. "Nothing bad at any rate. Hopefully lots of good stuff."

"What I mean is," she lowered her voice, "make sure you guys use a condom."

"Georgia!" Macy made a face. "Of course we will."

"Have fun then." They hugged and headed back to the two men, who were still chatting with one another.

"I'll call you tomorrow," Macy said over her shoulder as she and Mr. Muscles walked away.

"You were about to tell me," Shale began but was interrupted.

"Hiya!" It was a really cute brunette. She wore a tiny skirt and the highest heels Georgia had ever seen. She was smiling up at Shale, who… He didn't react actually. Why not? She would have expected something from the guy, since the woman standing in front of him was mighty cute. It didn't look like she was wearing a bra. Either that, or it was really cold in there and well, yeah, since it *wasn't cold there was no other explanation for the perky nips. "I'm Cheryl and you are?" Short-skirt fluttered her lashes. When Shale didn't answer she went on. "Can I get you a drink?" More fluttering.*

Georgia took a small step back. This was the part where she left them to it. Shale was looking for a good time. This was his chance.

Georgia was shocked when Shale shook his head. "My girlfriend might not like that very much." He put an arm around Georgia's shoulders. Say what? *She was too startled to do anything but stand there, mouth gaping a little. Georgia had been so sure he would accept the offer of a drink.*

The brunette had wide blue eyes and full, glossy lips. She was pushing out her chest as if continued world peace depended on it.

"Oh." Short-skirt looked at her like the concept of Shale being with her was crazy. All wide-eyed and puzzled. She even gave Georgia the once-over, a frown appearing as she did. "I thought you were one of the guys in town for one night."

"I am. I brought my girlfriend along." His arm tightened around her. He smelled amazing. Clean and manly. So good. He was warm too. Really warm.

"Okay. I see." She made a face. "I didn't think she looked much like she was with you," she mumbled. This time she gave Georgia a dirty look.

What the…?

She might be a freckly ginger with a little junk in the trunk, but she didn't deserve that kind of a reaction. "Well, we are *together. Very much so!"*

Short-skirt's expression just got a whole lot nastier.

Georgia felt her blood heat. "My man happens to love tits and ass with a side of sass. We're very much in love, so you can beat it." She wasn't sure what came over her when she got up onto her tippy-toes and kissed Shale. She didn't just kiss him. She went all possessive on him as well. Staked a claim! Big time! Georgia covered his mouth with hers. She stuck her tongue into his mouth, then grabbed his bicep with her free hand and put her arm around him with the other. Still clutching her wine.

Good lord!

His muscles were thick and hard. She may have moaned just then. In fact, she did moan… loudly. They kept at it for a good long minute. Long after the brunette had left. Georgia didn't have to check. Short-skirt would be long gone. A kiss like the one they were sharing couldn't be faked, even if everything else was. It was hot. It was heavy. It had her nipples tightening and other places tingling.

She was out of breath when he finally broke the kiss. He broke the kiss. Not her. She'd still be pressed tightly against him, her tongue dancing with his, if he hadn't.

A smile toyed with the side of his mouth. His full sexy mouth. The mouth she was staring at right then. Almost in awe. "Do you want to get out of here?" he asked.

CHAPTER 5

*S*hale watched her sober up in an instant. Her eyes went from hazy and lust-drunk to bright and… Was that fear that flashed in their depths?

The female let him go and even took a step back. "I can't." She shook her head. "I have work in the morning. A ton of work. I'm getting up early and…," She swallowed. "I can't, that's all."

He smiled. "I might need to head back to the hotel to change my shirt." Shale turned, giving her a view of his back.

When he turned back, she was clutching a hand to her mouth. Her eyes were wide. "Oh no," she said through her hand, her words muffled. "I'm sorry," she added, after taking her hand away. "Shit!" She looked down at her now empty wine glass. "I'm such a klutz."

"Here…" she closed the space between them and gripped his forearm, "turn back around."

She gasped. Even though she hadn't meant it like that, the sound was still amazing to his ears. His balls tightened up some. He wanted to hear her gasp like that when his cock was buried inside *her. Deep inside her.*

"You're really wet," she said.

Words he wanted to whisper to her.

"I didn't think I had that much left in my glass," she went on, "I need to find a dishcloth." Before he could stop her, she headed to the bar, returning minutes later with a soda in one hand and a cloth in her other.

"It's not the end of the world," he said, noting the determination in her eyes.

"I feel awful. I think I ruined your shirt."

He shrugged. "It's just a shirt."

"It looks expensive. Designer. That..." she pointed at the embroidered logo on the pocket, "logo looks familiar. I'm sure it's designer."

It was. It had cost a fortune. It didn't matter. Not in the least.

"It'll wash out and even if it doesn't. I don't really care." He looked back over his shoulder at the red stain. He didn't give a shit. So what! "I don't like wearing shirts much anyway."

Her eyes brightened up a whole lot. She licked her lips and glanced down at his chest before looking back up at him. They were a touch hazy. Very beautiful. A gorgeous green. Only highlighted by her wild tumble of hair. A fiery, startling red he wanted to fist in his hands while fucking—

"Turn around." Her voice was no-nonsense and commanding. Fuck if he didn't like it a whole damn lot. He did as she said.

"Now hold still." She got to work on his shirt.

Shale held up his hands. "I really don't mind—"

"Well, you should, because I don't think this is coming out." She sounded so wound up.

"It's okay," he tried, but her wiping only got more frantic. She stopped to soak the cloth with more club soda. "I mean it," he added.

"I don't care about the shirt." Shale turned and took the cloth and soda from her hands. He placed them on a nearby table, quickly turning back to face her.

She looked upset, a deep frown marred her forehead. "I'm so sorry. I'm such a klutz. I—"

Shale gripped his shirt in both hands and pulled. There was a tearing noise as he ripped his shirt open. Buttons went flying. The female's jaw dropped. "There," he chuckled. "Problem solved. The stain doesn't matter anymore."

She opened and closed her mouth a couple of times, her eyes on his chest... then on his abs... and back up to his chest. Her gaze slid slowly back down... down... back to his abs and lower to where his dick was hardening up. How could it not? This delectable female happened to be fucking the hell out of him with her eyeballs.

Shale closed the space between them and put his hands on her hips. Her lovely full hips. 'Tits and ass with a side of sass' was true. Only, she was sweet and shy as well. Such a fantastic combination. "I don't give a shit about the shirt. I'd trade ten like it for another kiss. Come back to the hotel with me," he asked.

"You don't waste any time, do you?"

"I'm only here for one night, so... no." He shook his head.

She frowned. "Why the urgency? Do you have a girlfriend or a wife back home?"

Shale shook his head. "No! I'm single. I would never fuck around on someone."

She looked around them, probably noting how several females were standing close by... watching... waiting. "You do know that you could have your pick of women in this place." She scrunched up her nose.

"I happen to want you." He kept his eyes on her.

"Just like that."

"Just like that." He cupped her chin in his hand and listened as her heart-rate sped up. *"Believe it or not, I don't fuck around all that much."*

"Much?" She raised her brows.

He smiled. *"I didn't say that I never fuck around."* Because of those bastard hunters, it had been almost a year since his last Stag Run. It might be just as long before his next one. *"It doesn't happen all that often, and most females don't interest me."*

She raised her brows. *"Oh? Why's that?"*

He shrugged. *"I'm picky. I'll admit it."* He let her go.

"And you want me... is that it?"

"Yes." He nodded. *"You're having a hard time with that part and I'm not sure why. You're very sexy. Although we haven't talked for very long, I can tell you're intelligent as well."*

"It's such a pity I have so much work to get through or I might be tempted. That kiss was..." She bit down on her lower lip. *"It was great."*

Shale leaned in close, almost touching her. *"It sure was."* He paused. *"I want to kiss you a whole lot more, and not necessarily on the lips."* He spoke into the shell of her ear, noting how she broke out in gooseflesh. Her scent grew more intoxicating. Coconut with a hint of fruit. He wasn't sure which kind, only that it made his mouth water for a taste.

She inhaled sharply. *"Again, I'm tempted but—"*

"But nothing! Forget about work. Forget about... whatever it is that's got you so bogged down."

She sucked in a breath, probably to deny it.

"I can tell," he went on. *"There's a lot going on in that mind of yours. You look tense, seriously wound up, and I can help you with that."*

She chuckled. *"Oh, really now?"*

"Yes, really."

"You having sex with me will make all my troubles go away? Make them all disappear?" She laughed some more.

"For a couple of hours, at least. Hell, I'll make you forget your own name. I'll make you come so many times you'll turn into a puddle of jello. You won't be able to be anything other than relaxed. My mouth and my hands will know every inch of your body. My cock—"

"You can stop right there!" Her heart was racing. He could scent her arousal, despite all the patrons and warring scents in the place.

"You pretty much had me when you tore open your shirt."

He choked out a laugh. "I did?"

"Pretty much, yes. You have a good chest… and your abs aren't too bad either. And ripping your shirt half off to prove a point was… a sweet thing to do. So, you're here for one night only?"

"One night only." He nodded once, holding up a finger.

"So, no exchanging of numbers? No ties, or tomorrows, or any of that?"

Had he read this wrong? Was she more interested than she let on? Was she looking for a relationship? It hadn't seemed that way. "No. If that bothers you then—"

"No!" She shook her head.

Thank fuck!

"One night only would work best for me. I'm… not in a place in my life where anything more than that would be remotely possible. I don't want to know anything about you. I'm not going to tell you anything about me. We need to get that out of the way up front. I don't want to know what you do for a living, or what your favorite food is."

"Works for me." He took her hand in his. "You ready to go, or do you want to stay for another drink?"

She widened her eyes. "Have another drink so that we can have deep meaningful conversations? I don't think so."

"We could find things to talk about. General stuff. I could tell you what I plan on doing to you later."

Her cheeks flushed and her breathing picked up a whole lot. Good!

"I'd rather you showed me." She smiled. It was shy and so fucking sexy. He actually felt excited for what was to come. He'd been going on Stag Runs for many years. This feeling was rare.

"I don't do this kind of thing very often… Okay, I don't do this kind of thing ever. I've never done anything like this before."

He nodded once. "I got that impression. That's fine." He squeezed her hand, hoping she wasn't going to change her mind.

"I'm not sure when last I shaved," she muttered, half to herself, her cheeks turning pink. "I think I shaved under my arms the other day, but I can't be—"

"I don't give a shit!" He cupped her face and kissed her again. Shale didn't waste any time, he went straight for it. Hot and hard. Her mouth was soft. Her body even softer. He wrapped a hand in her hair, giving it a light tug.

She moaned, deep. His balls pulled tight. His dick woke up. "Let's get out of here?" he said as soon as he pulled away.

She nodded. "Yes, let's."

He took her hand in his and led the way. Eager for what was to come. More excited than a kid on Christmas morning. "Just one thing before we go." He turned back to her. "Do you remember my name?"

"I do." She smiled. "It's Shale."

"Good. You need to know what to scream later." He winked at her, eliciting a giggle. "Um…" Now for the hard part. Hopefully she didn't slap him. "I can't remember your name. I know you *introduced yourself earlier but…" He grit his teeth for a moment.*

"It doesn't matter." She shook her head. "You can call me… Red." She touched her hair.

"Not very imaginative. I think I'd rather know your actual name."

She shook her head slowly. "Nope. It's better if you didn't."

"I won't stalk you or anything. I promise." This was a woman after his own heart. It didn't matter that he didn't know her name. Not even a little bit, and yet, he wanted to know. He could see she wasn't going to budge. "It's a state. I remember that much. Fuck if I can remember which one."

"It doesn't matter. You can call me whatever you want."

"I wouldn't mind knowing your name, though. Just your name." Damn, but he was starting to sound like a pussy. "No need for a surname. No need for any other information swapping."

She just stared up at him with those gorgeous green eyes.

"Is it Carolina… Caroline! It's Caroline," he blurted.

She laughed and shook her head.

"Texas… your name is Texas, isn't it? Odd name but… we'll go with it."

She laughed even harder and he found himself loving it. It seemed he could help her unwind using more than just his dick. Made him feel… good.

"Montana… no… no… Dakota? It's Dakota, right?"

She shook her head, still laughing her ass off. "I'm not telling you either way."

"How about Alabama?"

She smiled, biting down on her lip.

"If you don't tell me, I'm calling you by every state there is. That way I will have covered them all by the end of the night and will have called you by your name at least once."

Her smile widened and something flared in her eyes. *"You know every state by heart?"*

"I do... at least, I'm pretty sure I do."

"Okay, then."

"Okay, Alabama... let's go." He squeezed her hand.

CHAPTER 6

Shale was just as she remembered him, tall, dark and absurdly gorgeous. The last only incensed her more. *Bastard!* His eyes widened as they landed on her belly. She could see his mind work.

Yes asshole, this is exactly the way it looks!

She almost felt like laughing while she watched him shit his pants. Not literally of course, but it wasn't far off. She made her way over, hating how he just got better looking the closer she drew to him. His casual button-down shirt fit him just so. His jeans as well. Shale was tall and built and a complete jerk.

She wasn't just thinking that because a blonde had just stopped in front of him. The woman said something to Shale, who ignored her flat. His eyes stayed glued to Georgia's.

Well, unlucky for him… it looked like she was just about to rain on his parade. The blonde said something else. Probably trying to buy Shale a drink. Trying to pick him up, more like. If she waited five minutes for Georgia to say what she needed to say, the blonde could have him.

The guy standing next to Shale spoke to the blonde. "I'm Stone," he said, smiling. "It's... to meet you. Can... get... drink?" she managed to hear him say.

She closed the last remaining space, all the emotion and all of the fear from the last few months welling up inside her. "You asshole!" Georgia yelled.

She ignored the blonde who was now looking at her. Everyone in the vicinity was looking at her like she'd lost her mind. The blonde said something she couldn't make out.

Shale's friend chuckled. "I hope this isn't what I think it is."

It most certainly damn well was!

Shale didn't say anything. He looked pale. His eyes went from her belly to her face and back again. His jaw was tight. Shale's friend and the blonde walked away.

"You said I couldn't get pregnant," she blurted, her eyes narrowing on him. May as well get it out in the open. "You said it wouldn't happen. You said you were clean and that you were sterile." She waved an accusing finger. "Does this look like sterile to you?" She pointed at her distended belly. "I'm such an idiot," she muttered, more to herself. The condom had broken. Go freaking figure. No sex for almost two years and the condom broke with Pinocchio over here. Just her luck!

"No." He shook his head. "It can't be." He shook it harder, looking completely confused and bewildered. Georgia wasn't really sure what there was to be bewildered about. Sex sometimes led to pregnancy. It was how it worked. Then again, she had been shocked too when she had finally plucked up the courage to do a test. Shale had been really believable when he'd told her not to worry about becoming pregnant. Maybe he really thought he couldn't have kids. She'd been such an idiot.

Shale scratched his chin, still looking like he couldn't fathom how this was happening. Unless he really had thought he was sterile, in which case, he was about to accuse her of lying. She needed to get this over with and to get out of this bar.

"This is the part where you deny being the father." *Typical! Why did she feel so darned disappointed?* "Well listen up, bucko, you are the only guy I've had sex with in a very long time. You and only you." She jabbed a finger into his chest. His very chiseled chest. The fact that she even thought that last thought made her angry as all hell. "I left with you that night because I knew you wouldn't be interested in a relationship. You can relax, I'm not here to try to trap you or anything. I still don't want a relationship." She remembered how her last one had ended. Nope, no relationship for her for a good long while, maybe ever. *No thanks.* Georgia felt her eyes well with tears. She blamed it firmly on the hormones, quickly blinking them away. "I'm not ready to be a mother... I'm not..." It didn't matter what she wanted. It just wasn't possible. "I can't raise... can't possibly...I just can't do this!" She handed him her telephone number on a piece of paper. "Here."

Shale was still frowning, he took it and read it.

"My number," she said, unnecessarily. "I'm due in three months. You have that long to decide if you want to raise this child." She touched her belly. Maybe he wouldn't turn out to be a colossal jerk. Maybe—*No!* Better not to think along those lines. Chances were good that the Joyces would get this baby as planned. "Otherwise, it looks like I might have a great family lined up to adopt this baby. I can't keep it." She sniffed, trying hard not to cry. "I wish things were different but I… um… I just can't." She sniffed again. Damn, she needed to get out of there before she blubbered like an idiot.

Georgia turned and walked towards the door. She didn't look back. It seemed to take an age to negotiate her way through all the people. She pushed the door open, hearing it shut behind her. Georgia leaned against the wall, gulping in air.

"And?" Macy asked. "How did he take it?"

She tried to smile. "He was shocked. Didn't say much of anything. Then again, I didn't give him too much of a chance."

"And now?" Macy raised her brows.

Georgia snorted. "Now I head home."

"Just like that?"

She nodded. "Yep, just like that. He has my number. If he calls, I'll be surprised. He's such a player. There is no way he's cut out to be a father. I'd be so shocked if he called, I'd probably drop my phone. Heck," she smiled, feeling some of the tension drain, "I'd eat my hat… the—" Georgia noticed that Macy was looking at something behind her. Something over Georgia's shoulder. She felt her back prickle. Her friend was staring at the entrance to the bar. The one Georgia had just left. The one through which noise was blaring. Like the door was ajar. *Oh god!*

She squeezed her eyes shut for a second. "He's behind me, isn't he?"

Macy cringed and nodded. "I'm afraid so."

"It's a pity you're not wearing a hat," his deep smoky voice sounded behind her, "or I'd make you eat it."

"This is my cue to leave." Macy smiled. "I think the two of you have a lot to talk about. You call me if you need me."

"I will." Georgia watched as Macy walked away. Then she slowly turned, facing Shale. He no longer looked gobsmacked. His stance was relaxed at first glance, but upon looking closer, his shoulders were tight. His golden eyes seemed to look right through her. No, not through her, into her, like he was trying to find answers without using words.

His nostrils flared once and then a second time. "Can we go somewhere to talk?" he finally asked.

"Why?" She didn't want to be funny, or unkind, or come across as cold, but she had limited time. She should have already been in bed. Also, this seemed a waste of time. "We both know you're not father material. I told you about this as a courtesy. It was the right thing to do. It's *my* problem though. I'll handle it. This child will have a good life." She put her hand on her belly. "I can't raise him or her, but I will make sure this baby will want for nothing. I can promise you that. So, you can turn around and walk back in there. I'm sure you had a whole lot of fun planned for this evening. Just be a little more careful this time. You definitely have swimmers."

"For the record, I never told you I was sterile." Shale still couldn't believe this was happening. He took a step towards her, inhaling her scent again. Not that he had to. Now that they were outside, he could pick up on how it had changed. It was subtle but there.

She was indeed pregnant by a shifter. *His whelps.* His heart raced all over again. His palms felt instantly clammy.

She narrowed her eyes. Not buying a word of it. "You said I couldn't get pregnant. You convinced me of it. I'm such an idiot," she muttered the last, to herself. Her eyes were even bigger than he remembered.

"I'm sorry." He shook his head, wiped a hand across his forehead. "I can't believe this is happening. I shouldn't have said that. I was sure though." The female hadn't been in heat. He had been able to scent that.

"How the hell could you have been so sure? You just said you aren't sterile, so that doesn't make sense." She put her hands on her hips. "Look," she shook her head, "it doesn't matter anymore. I *did* become pregnant. I should have known better. I'm pissed at you, but I'm ultimately really angry with myself."

Shale liked her. There it was. This female. Mother of his whelps… His heart sped right up. He liked her even if he still couldn't remember her name… not her real name. It had been fun calling her by every state in the book that night. He had a feeling it wouldn't go over so well right then. "Just go, okay? I give you permission to leave right now and to never turn back." She waved a hand. "To go on with your life. I will make sure this baby is well taken care of."

"You just said you weren't… keeping the baby." *Babies.*

Shit! She had no clue she was pregnant with twins.

She shook her head. "I've found a great couple. I requested visitation. I've insisted that regular scheduled visits be included in the adoption contract. I won't just abandon him or her." He watched how she caressed her belly. He doubted that she even knew she was doing it. The female sucked in a deep breath, trying to keep her emotions in check. He registered sadness in her eyes.

"If you turn around and walk away now, I'll pretend I never saw you. In so doing you can deny paternity. That will be that, free and clear."

Shale pulled in a deep breath. "I don't want to be free and clear."

Her jaw dropped open. This was the last thing she expected to hear. Why was that so hard to fathom?

"Okay, that's fine but if you want to be a father to this child… if…" She stopped talking, her eyes flicking to the side and back. She had never even thought of the possibility this would happen. It hadn't crossed her mind. She looked like a duck out of water. "Do you actually want to raise this child? Is that what you are saying?" She sounded completely shocked at the prospect.

"No." He shook his head.

Her shoulders actually relaxed. "That's what I thought. So, you're walking away, then?" She nodded, like she was resigning herself to the fact. Like it made more sense that way.

"No, I'm not walking away." He shook his head, keeping his eyes on her. "That's just it. *I'm* not going to raise this child, *we're* going to raise the baby. *We*." He could tell that she loved this baby… *babies. Shit!* He needed to sit down with her and to have a long conversation.

"That's sweet."

"I mean it."

She choked out a laugh. "I work two jobs, Shale. I have responsibilities. I won't be any kind of a mother to this baby. I can barely feed myself. I have a plan, okay?"

"Plans change. I'm here now... I'm..." He looked around them. "You're not alone in this. Not anymore."

She scrutinized him. "Just like that?" She clicked her fingers.

"Yes, just like that. Why is that so hard to believe?"

"You're a player. You like to have one-night stands. You were just in there on the prowl. You like partying and... you don't want to be tied down. I can tell."

"Actually, I don't sleep with loads of women. I told you that the first time we met." All true. On occasion with the unmated dragon females but, otherwise, only on Stag Runs which happened every six months – if they were lucky. "You don't know me either, so it isn't fair to judge me."

"I know your type, Shale, and only too well. You couldn't even remember my name that night."

"That's not fair!" He ran a hand through his hair. "You only told us that once, when you were introducing yourself to Rock"

"If you had been as interested as you said you were, you would have remembered."

"I was interested! Surely you knew that. I had hoped I'd made that part clear." Just like the kiss, the rutting had been off the damned charts.

Her pupils dilated. Was she also thinking back on that

night? "Still," she shrugged, "I didn't care much at the time that you couldn't remember but..."

"I know it's the name of a state. I don't know which one." He sounded exasperated because he was. "I wish you would have told me." He meant it too. He'd thought about this female a good number of times after that night. More than he normally thought back on females. He had often found himself wondering what her name was.

She rolled her eyes. "I wasn't looking for anything other than a good time with you. That much was mutual. This," she pointed at her belly, "wasn't supposed to happen."

"It has, though."

"I know that!" Her voice was animated. "Of course, I realize that! I've done nothing but think about it for months. I just can't wrap my head around you wanting to raise this child... with me. I'm a complete stranger."

"We'll get to know each other."

"I can't stop working. Didn't you hear that part?"

"I told you that you're not alone anymore. I'll help out. I'm not a deadbeat. I might be a lot of things but I'm not that. I can tell you care about this baby. Our baby." His throat clogged as he said it. Shale took a second to compose himself. "That you would like nothing better than to be a mother to this child." He looked down at her well-rounded belly. His whelps. He still couldn't believe it. Shale wasn't sure whether he wanted to put his to ear to her stomach or to run away. He took a small step closer.

"Of course, I care." Her voice was raised, and determination shone in her eyes. "I care very much. If things were different... I..." She wiped a hand over her face, looking tired. "I'm glad you want to be a father to this baby. I'm happy you want us to raise him or her but it's not going to be possible." She shook her head. "Unless you make decent money as… I don't have a clue what you do. I don't know anything about you." She looked at her watch. "It's late. I have work in the morning. We can talk again in a couple of days."

Then she was turning to leave. Shale was losing her and quite possibly his whelps as well. It looked like she had made her mind up about where this was going. This, despite what she had said earlier.

"I have money," he blurted. Okay, he hadn't meant to say that.

Shale expected her to perk up. To smile. To hug him. Maybe he'd expected her to relax at the prospect.

She barely turned back and even took another step away from him. "Okay," she nodded. "As I said, we'll discuss it."

"You won't have to work. I'll cover—"

"Hold up." She put her hand up. "This is happening too quickly." She shook her head. "I'm not just giving up my work. I told you I have responsibilities. Big ones. I don't know you at all. Forgive me but," she winced, "I don't trust you, Shale. We can talk about it. Maybe we can work something out. Right now—"

"Let's go for coffee? One quick cup. There are a couple of things I need to tell you. It's important."

She smiled. It lasted all of a second. "I don't drink coffee at the moment. Caffeine isn't good for the baby."

Something in his chest clenched. She was already such a good mother. Fuck if that didn't make him feel something. Exactly what that something was, he couldn't say. "Um... okay... tea then... herbal?"

"I need to get home. I'm cold and tired and... a little overwhelmed. You have my number." She looked down at the paper still clenched in his hand.

"Tomorrow then?" he asked, sounding desperate. He didn't give a shit. "Can we meet and talk? Surely you need to take a break at some point?"

She nodded once. "Call me. I'll make time. We can talk about it."

"Tomorrow?"

She gave him the ghost of a smile and nodded once before turning and leaving.

CHAPTER 7

The next day…

Georgia struggled to concentrate on the screen for even a second longer. She rubbed her eyes, trying to dispel some of the heaviness. *No luck!* It didn't help that she'd been up for what felt like half the night, the night before. She couldn't fall asleep. It didn't matter how tired she was. She was just too wired. Georgia couldn't get the events from the previous evening out of her mind. She finally managed to pass out in the early hours of the morning. The droning sound of the alarm had hurt when it went off. Not being able to have any coffee had hurt even more.

Shale had contacted her at eight that morning. Georgia wasn't sure what to make of the whole thing. He seemed eager. There was part of her that had woken up excited. There was a part of her that had woken up with hope. It scared her. She didn't want to feel excited or hopeful. It was dangerous to allow those emotions to creep in, but what if... what if he was serious about them raising the baby? Not as a couple but as a father and mother who both cared and who both contributed. Would it work? Could it? Dare she even think along those lines.

It was too soon.

Far too soon to say. She needed to calm herself down. The fact of the matter was, she had no idea who Shale was. Not really. Maybe he was the kind of guy who made rash decisions and then regretted them. Maybe he wasn't someone you could count on. He could be a huge liar. Then again maybe he was the opposite of all those things. Maybe he *was* father material.

Stop!

Georgia saved the cover she was working on. It was for a particularly difficult romance author. She liked the guys on the cover to be both buff and good-looking. Not an easy ask. In the end, Georgia had ended up meshing two guys. The image needed more work. She'd tackle it after her meeting with Shale. Hopefully, she'd be able to think a little more clearly then.

Irritatingly, she found herself applying make-up. Why? She was meeting Shale for tea at one of the local coffee shops in town. It was nothing. They needed to talk, and yet there she was applying lip gloss and mascara. It wasn't like Shale was going to look at her like that, in this state, and even if she wasn't pregnant, she shouldn't care about how Shale looked at her, period. He wasn't even her type, beyond that one night. Sure, he was gorgeous, but that's where his attributes ended. He had been sweet, though, that night. And funny. But mainly really sweet. Probably because he wanted to get in her pants. It hadn't been just that, had it? Georgia pushed out a breath, thinking back on their time together.

The drive to the hotel lasted all of a few minutes. Shale swiped his key card in the slot while Georgia quickly typed a message to Macy, telling her friend where she was. Namely, in the same hotel block. At least, this way, if something sinister happened to her, Macy would know where she was and who she was with. Not that she was afraid, although maybe she should be. Shale was huge. He wasn't scary in the least, though.

He had held her hand on the way to his car. A big, black SUV. He'd helped her in and hadn't touched her once since leaving the bar. Not so much as a finger. He stepped to the side, giving her space to enter his hotel room. "Are you sure you wouldn't rather go back to your place?" His deep voice was loud in the empty hallway. "You seem nervous."

"I am… just a little. It's not you or anything. Like I said earlier, I don't normally do things like this."

"Your place then, instead? Maybe you'll feel more comfortable?" He raised his brows.

She shook her head. Georgia would rather he didn't know where she stayed. This was neutral ground. It might also be because she didn't want him to see her tiny apartment and her threadbare sofa. Her sheets were a horrible, faded yellow. It had been a year or more since they were a crisp white. "This is fine." She smiled.

"Probably better." He threw her a cocky smile.

"How so?" she asked, looking at him skeptically. Where was he going with this?

Shale leaned forward just a little. "We wouldn't want your neighbors to hear you screaming. They'd never look at you the same again."

Her mouth fell open for a second. Then she scowled at him.

"Screaming? I'm not sure I like where this is going. At least my neighbors would call the cops if you were—"

"Not that kind of screaming, Texas. I assure you." He leaned a little closer still.

She could feel his heat. Her mouth felt dry all of a sudden. "Oh… um… I think I know what you're trying to tell me." She licked her lips, her nerves hitting her hard.

"No pressure," he quickly added. "We don't have to do anything if—"

It wasn't easy considering how damn tall he was, but she reached up and planted her lips on his. He groaned and circled his arms around her.

He broke the kiss. "Yeah, we could make out. That would be good too." He picked her up. As in, off the ground. It didn't seem like it was any effort to him at all. His tongue clashed with hers and another zing of lust rushed through her. It emanated from her clit and spread out through her body. She clutched his biceps. They were thick and hard, like the rest of him. It had been so long since she had been touched like this. Too long. Her nerve-endings were already firing on all cylinders and he had hardly done anything yet. Make that, he hadn't done anything yet. What had she signed up for? Possibly more than she could handle.

He walked her into the hotel room, in his arms. Carrying. Her. The door closed behind them with a soft click.

"Let's sit here," he said between kisses.

Georgia cracked open her eyes. "Holy shit!" she breathed out the words rather than said them. They were high up. Then again, the elevator had gone up and up. She'd been too busy with that text to Macy to take much notice. The view was stunning. Who knew little Dalton Springs, lit up at night, could look so good? Beyond the town was mostly black. And then there was the moon. Large and round, hanging from the sky. Also, this was more of an apartment than a hotel room. They were in the living area. Shale was about to lower them onto the sofa.

"Wouldn't a bed be better?" Her voice had a desperate edge, but she was feeling too aroused to care. She pulled back so that she could look him in the eyes. Well, sort of look him in the eyes. Shale hadn't turned the lights on, so she could barely see, but she could make out his face. She could feel his breath mingle with hers as well. His chest heaved against her. "Kissing sounds great, but I also want some good old-fashioned sex, so I think that maybe the bedroom would be better." A jumble of words. She'd never felt more nervous in her life. "Although I might miss that view."

"I'll give you something else to look at." Then he chuckled. "That came out sounding corny."

She laughed as well.

"I'm thankful we're on the same page here. I want sex as well. So badly! I also want you happy and at ease. There is no pressure."

"I am at ease." Her words were still breathless. How could they not be, she had her arms around his shoulders. His very broad shoulders. Shale was sweet for a player. It was unexpected. He started walking.

"We'll take it slow," he murmured against her lips before taking back her mouth. "At least at first."

"Good, because I think I want hard and fast." Where did that come from? She wasn't normally this bold. Her clit throbbed at the groan that came from him. It had a growly edge that did it for her.

"Shit." He put her down on the bed. "You are so fucking gorgeous, Iowa."

She giggled. "Not that you can see me. It's pitch-black in here." She leaned back with her hands on the bed behind her.

She could hear Shale walk along the side of the bed. There was a clicking noise and soft light filled the tiny space. It was beautiful. A huge bed. *Big fluffy pillows. White bedding and sheets.* White!

"You like the room?" he asked.

"Yes, it's amazing. All for a martial arts convention." She whistled.

He shrugged. "We got a good deal because there are so many of us."

Shale smiled. *Those dimples.* Oh, lord. *Then he removed his torn shirt and all she could focus on was his abs and that V thing just above his low-riding jeans. Oh, and the bulge in those jeans. It was big, he was really big. Everywhere. She wanted him. If she was honest with herself, she had since she had first seen him. He toed off his boots and began to unclasp his jeans.*

"Wait." She put up a hand. "Stop," she added on a whisper.

He turned serious. *That burning in his eyes instantly extinguished.* "Have you changed your mind? It's okay if you have."

She shook her head. "I want to do it." *She pointed at his pants, feeling her mouth curve into a smile. She was feeling wicked. That, and very bold. You would think she'd had more to drink than just half a glass of wine.*

Shale looked down at the ground for a beat before locking eyes with her, his sexy mouth was curved into a seductive smile. "You want to undress me?" *He raised his brows, looking hotter than anything or anyone she had ever seen before. Ever.*

She nodded. *Georgia so wanted to do it for him. There was something freeing about this. She was never going to see Shale again.*

He grinned. "Well, okay then." *He moved to stand in front of her.*

Georgia just stood there for a few seconds taking him in. All of him. Every hard line. She eventually gripped the top button in her fingers, which shook just a little. Nerves and excitement all rolled into one.

His throat worked as she began to pluck each one open. Georgia *slowly slid his jeans down. It was like unwrapping a present. A long-awaited gift… just for her. His shaft sprang free.*

Oh, man.

Commando! *His penis was a thing of beauty. Long and thick. It slanted a little to the left. His head was large. As in triple-XL. For once in her life, she was thankful for being a little bigger than most girls. She wouldn't break easily.*

A surge of need tugged at her and she rose up, taking his head into her mouth. It just happened. Again. She wasn't sure what had come over her. She and Tate had dated for weeks before they'd had sex for the first time. It had been two or three months before she'd plucked up the courage to give him head. It wasn't something she enjoyed, and yet, right then, in that moment, all she wanted was to suck Shale off. To hear him groan. To watch him tense up and his eyes squeeze shut. To feel him vibrate with need. She took him deeper in her mouth. The taste of salty pre-come hit her tongue. Oh god, even his come tasted good. This guy was too much and not nearly enough.

Shale cursed softly and cupped her cheeks. "No," he growled. She was forced to release him with a soft pop. "We'll save that for later, Kentucky." He bobbed his brow, his smile was tense and needy. "I won't last with your mouth on me. I haven't fucked in a while. I'm…" He groaned, low and deep. "My balls are already in my throat from wanting you so badly. I think I'll save it for when I'm buried deep inside you." His eyes smoldered.

That was both the dirtiest and sexiest thing anyone had ever said to her. She swallowed hard and nodded once.

"Can I undress you *now?" he asked, his gaze hesitant. His eyes had a soft look of concern. The rest of him was tense with need. His cock jutted from between his hips. Shale kicked his own jeans the rest of the way off as he spoke.*

She nodded and then laughed when he lifted his eyes to the ceiling

and said a prayer of thanks. He was so cute and sweet and sexy…
and hung like an ox.

"Don't run away screaming when you see my hairy legs." Her
voice quivered a little. Georgia had felt bold not a minute ago. Right
then, not so much. What if he didn't like what he saw? It was a
possibility. A guy like this probably only ever slept with supermodels.
She wondered, for the tenth time, why he had picked her up.

Shale sat down next to her. He hooked an arm around her waist.
"I told you I don't give a shit about any of that. I want to look at
you… every last inch of you." He dropped a kiss on the side of her
mouth.

Oh, god help her. This piece of man-perfection wanted to look at
her. "Um… sheew… every inch, huh?" No. No. No. "Look, I'm
curvy. More curvy than most of the women in that bar. That means
I have…" She'd been about to say stretchmarks and cellulite, but he
interrupted her before she could do so.

Shale growled. "I had noticed your curves. Believe me on that one,
Nevada." He winked at her. "I think that you're sexy as fuck."
His voice was deep and gravely. Even more so than normal. His dick
jutted out from between his thighs. His muscular thighs. This guy
worked out. A lot.

"I don't exercise. At all," she blurted, wishing she could take it
back when she saw his eyes narrow. She felt like such an idiot. She
was supposed to take this sexy guy home and screw his brains out,
leaving before sunrise without a care in the world for a few short
hours. Yet, here she was second-guessing herself. Shale hadn't signed
up for this. He wasn't a shrink. What was wrong with her? Why
didn't she just take her clothes off and go at it? So what if he had
second thoughts. She wasn't having any. No way!

"I don't care about any of that. I'm very attracted to you. Look
at me." He glanced down. "I'm feeling a little apprehensive myself."

"You are?" That couldn't be true.

His eyes locked back with hers. "I'm not sure I'm going to last very long buried inside you." His jaw tightened. "I might just embarrass myself."

Her cheeks heated. He was sweet. Not at all what she expected.

"I want you, Kansas, you." He smiled. "I might not know your actual name, but I know that much. Do you understand that?" He made a soft noise of frustration. "I think that you are beautiful and sexy." His hand slipped beneath her shirt, but he kept it on her back. His fingers felt hot against her skin. "I love your wild tangle of hair. Your eyes are beautiful. I know for a fact that I'm going to love everything you are hiding beneath these clothes. Fucking love." He kissed her lips, softly and gently. "I happen to be a 'tits and ass' kind of a guy. If there's a side order of hips and thighs, all the better. You'll need to believe me on that."

His tongue breached her mouth and she kissed him back like her life depended on it. A deep rumble vibrated from his chest. Shale began to slowly lift her shirt and she must have tensed or something because he stopped.

He cupped her cheek with his big hand. "Let's make out. I'm sure I can make you come without taking any of your clothes off." He winked. "Multiple times."

Her pussy clenched. It all out clenched, and a zing of need rushed through her.

His nostrils flared and his eyes seemed to darken. "I mean it." His voice was deeper, so much more sexy. "We can take this slow. We don't even have to have sex." He said it like it pained him to get the words out.

"I definitely want sex. I'm sorry for being so…" She shrugged.

"You've never done this before. It's normal for you to be apprehensive." He paused. "I can see that you're stressed about something. I'm sure that's affecting you as well."

He was intuitive. "You're right, and I normally know someone *quite well before... I feel like an idiot." She rubbed her face.*

"It's important that you know that you're driving me crazy, Kentucky." He gave her a sexy half-smile that brought out his dimples. "Crazy." He widened his eyes and exhaled through his nose.

She giggled.

"Still haven't picked the right state yet, have I?"

She shook her head. "I'm not telling."

"I'm going to undress you now and I need you to know that I'm going to love everything I see."

"How can you possibly know that?" She felt her smile widen.

"Trust me, Virginia, I know! I'm taking off your clothes and then I'm going to go down on you. I am going to love tasting that sweet pussy of yours."

Oh, god.

Help me.

Kill me now.

Shale put a hand on her thigh and she almost jumped out of her skin. "I don't care about a bit of hair, and curves happen to be my favorite thing, along with redheads named after a state." He was so sweet. "Redheads who wreck shirts are my all-time and absolute favorite of them all."

She laughed. "You do know that only two percent of the world's population have red hair."

"Is that so, Tennessee?"

She nodded, still smiling. The muscles around her mouth actually hurt. It had been so long since she had smiled this much. Her muscles weren't used to it.

"Then you know my struggle is real." His eyes moved down the length of her. They heated as they did. His chest rose and fell in quick succession. He seemed genuinely attracted to her.

Georgia licked her lips. "You can undress me now." Her voice was steady. "Don't you dare laugh at my freckles… I have them everywhere. I'm also a natural redhead, so…"

CHAPTER 8

L augh?

What the fuck?

Someone had been feeding this female bullshit. He wanted to find the dickhead and put his fist down the male's throat. Shale had to force himself to unclench his fists. "There will be no laughing or running or anything other than staring because I am going to love the fuck out of your naked body. Look at me." *He wished he knew her real name. He wanted to look her in the eyes and say it. He wanted her to believe him enough to let him show her that he meant every word he was saying.* "Look at what you do to me." *He pointed to his hard-as-nails dick.* "I want you... just as you are."

She swallowed hard and nodded once. "Okay, then." She grabbed the hem of her shirt and pulled it over her head.

He kept his eyes on hers. Not wanting to scare her. "There," he pressed his lips to hers, whispering against them, "that wasn't so hard, was it?"

She shook her head. Shale kissed the hell out of her lips. Her soft, honeysuckle lips. He could kiss her all damned night. She allowed him to maneuver her so that she was lying down. He kept his weight on his arms, which he bracketed on either side of her. He kept his body, his cock, off her for now, not wanting to scare her. A dragon shifter dick, his dick, was a scary thing to a human female.

"Delicious," he murmured as he moved to kiss her neck. She arched into him and made a soft moaning noise. Her full breasts mashed up against his chest. He could feel her hard nipples through her bra.

"Can I touch you a little?"

"Mmm, what?" Her voice was dazed. Great! That meant she was relaxing. He hoped he hadn't screwed that up.

"I'd really like to cup those gorgeous breasts of yours. I've been working really hard at not ogling them… it tends to put females off."

She giggled.

"I'm sure you're used to males staring at your chest, instead of looking you in your eyes, gorgeous as they are."

She giggled louder, her body vibrating beneath him.

She kissed him, nipping at his lower lip. His hips thrust forward as her teeth touched his flesh. Fuck! He almost came right there and then. There was that sass, hidden beneath those layers of shyness.

"So, you like a little biting?" Her voice was husky.

"Very much." His mouth was still on hers. If only she knew who she was with. "You have no fucking idea how much, Nebraska."

"Nice to know. I'll try not to do it too hard."

"No such thing." He nuzzled into her neck.

"Let me…" He wasn't sure what she was talking about. But then she thrust her chest up into his, he heard a click and he felt her bra slip.

Shale moved back to her neck and nipped at the soft skin just below her ear. She moaned. He sucked on her lobe and she groaned. He could scent her need and it drove him wild. Moving slowly, he peppered kisses down her collarbone. Her heart-rate kicked up a notch or two. Her breath came out in little pants.

"Fuck me!" he growled, as he caught sight of her breasts. Two large mounds of utter perfection.

She covered them with her hands. The soft globes were still visible on either side of her fingers. This female was right on the money when she said she had curves. They were all in the right places. "They're probably a bit too big."

"No such thing, Florida." He shook his head.

"Definitely too freckly." She made a face. "My whole chest is freckly."

"Stop with that shit! I want to see you." He glanced up at her fearful expression. "I'm dying to suck on your nipples. You have no fucking idea how much." He sounded like an absolute pussy, but he didn't give a fuck. It was true. "I like the freckles too…" He looked down at her chest. At what he could see of it. His balls were tight. His dick throbbed. "I want to trace each one with my tongue and then suck on your hard little nubs."

When he looked up, her cheeks were flushed. "You do?"

"Oh, yes, Nevada!" He squeezed one eye shut. "Have I called you that already?"

She giggled and her breasts jiggled. He had to clench

his jaw to keep from coming like a teenager. "I don't remember right now."

He turned serious. "You have one of the best pairs of tits I've ever seen on a female."

She giggled harder. "That's so crass. I'm not sure if I should be offended."

"You should take it as a compliment because…" he tried.

"I'm not though, offended, because you're being really honest. I can see you mean it."

"I might be a lot of things, but I'm not a bullshitter."

"I'm beginning to see that." Her hands dropped to her sides, but he could see how tense she was. He hated the hell out of her insecurity. She was a beautiful female. Shale meant every word he had said to her.

He dropped his gaze to her chest, which rose and fell quickly. "Good lord!" he growled. "Pink and plump." He took one of her ripe nipples into his mouth and suckled.

She cried out as he nipped at her flesh. Then she groaned hard as he suckled on her a second time, a little harder this time. His other hand closed over the other orb. Too big for his hands. It was like Christmas had come early. He was one lucky son of a bitch. This female was perfection. Soft… so damned soft. Fuck! He growled against her flesh, eliciting another soft moan.

Shale lifted his head and looked up at her. Her eyes were pleasure-soaked and her cheeks were flushed.

"I'm going to take off these jeans now." He touched the top button of her pants.

She grit her teeth for half a beat, like she was wrestling with herself. "O-okay." She nodded. "It's just, I wasn't expecting this to happen. I—"

He kissed her. "Stop there. Nothing you say will put me off you."

"When I told you I hadn't shaved, well, I wasn't just talking about my legs. That's all I'm going to say on the matter." She lay back down, eyes wide and on the ceiling.

CHAPTER 9

S hale chuckled softly. His chest was against hers. He felt so good. She ran her hands down his back. His long, very muscular back. What was he doing there? With her? It was crazy. She half expected him to laugh and tell her it was all a mistake. Or a joke. Maybe this was all a dream.

Stop it!

She'd never had such confidence issues before. This was nuts. It needed to stop. Her ex had seriously messed with her mind. She couldn't let what had happened get to her like this. Heck, Georgia hadn't thought much about it. Tate had left because of what was going on with her mother. It had nothing to do with them as a couple. Or had it?

He put his forehead to hers for a second, bringing her back from her thoughts. "There is only one thing I like more than a redhead."

"And what is that?" She found herself smiling… again.

"Au-fucking-natural, Washington. Au-fucking-natural," he repeated, and sucked on her earlobe. Her clit throbbed. The bundle of nerves felt swollen and achy

"Good. Great because, well… because…" Oh hell! Why hadn't she taken care of business? Why? "I'm more than a little overgrown down there." She could physically feel her cheeks heat. "It's been two years since I… since my ex and I broke up and, well… I don't do this kind of thing, so naturally, I wasn't expecting to…"

Shale smiled. Those dimples. His gaze turned feral and the air froze in her lungs. "I love pussy hair. I fucking love it. Please tell me you're ginger everywhere. That you have freckles everywhere." He licked his lips.

She made a squeaking sound as she felt mortification flood her system. He didn't just say that. Please, no!

He whooped twice. "I'll take that as a yes, New York. I'm about to light you up like Times Square."

She threw her head back and laughed. "New York? Really? There isn't a chance in hell I'm named New York."

"I said I would work my way through them all and I plan on doing just that." His eyes stayed on hers. "Okay, so, I'm going to take your pants off now, and then I'm going to lick your clit until you come."

Shale didn't wait for a reply. She groaned as his hand closed over her mound. Every part of her was overly sensitive. Every nerve-ending was on high alert. Her body hummed with need. A finger… his thumb maybe, rubbed on her through her jeans and she wanted the barrier gone, as in yesterday. Oh, good lord!

"I can't wait to fuck you, Nevada." He was breathing hard, that hand of his rubbing up against her, seeming to know where she was most sensitive, even with a pair of jeans in the way. "I want to suck on your clit until you see stars." A harder rub against her sensitive nub had her moaning softly.

She was breathing hard. "Okay," she managed to grind out.

Another finger pushed against her opening. "I won't be gentle, I'm afraid. Have you been fucked hard before, Louisiana?" He somehow managed to rub both her clit and her channel. The need that coursed through her was almost excruciating.

Her back came off the bed. She instinctively tried to deepen the contact. "Mmmm… um… what was the question?" She groaned. His hand felt so good through her clothes.

"Do you like hard sex?"

"I think so…" she moaned. "Mmmm… hard sex."

Shale kissed her softly. Then his tongue was in her ear. Her groan was louder this time. He continued to rub on her through her jeans. Then his hand was inside her pants and she groaned so loudly, thankful they were at the hotel instead of at her house. The apartments on her block were cramped and close together. The walls were thin. Her neighbors would have heard all this, for sure. He dipped a finger inside her and she groaned again. Need coursed through her. It consumed every part of her. It made her want to rip her own clothes off and jump him like a cat in heat.

"You're so damned wet for me. Fuck!" He withdrew the hand and licked his finger. Licked.

It was the sexiest thing she had ever seen. His eyes closed in… ecstasy. He made a moaning noise as his lips smacked over his fingers. It turned her on even more.

Shale was both sweet and dirty. Really, really dirty. She never in her wildest dreams thought she would like that in a guy. She did though! Very much! Tate had been so reserved in bed. It was rare for him to want anything other than the missionary position. This was different. Good different.

"I need to be inside you now." He dipped down and sucked on her nipple, hard. His other hand tugged her jeans down. Then he kissed her belly and she had the urge to cover herself. He seemed to like her curves. His gaze was lust-filled. It helped in the confidence department. Georgia kicked off her pants, suddenly feeling another boost of confidence.

Shale ran his hands up and down her thighs. "Open up for me," he urged. "I want to see…" He groaned and gave a look that couldn't be faked. "That has to be just about the most gorgeous pussy I've ever seen."

She giggled. Georgia had never giggled this much in her life. She felt like a bit of a schoolgirl again.

Shale bit down on his lower lip for a second, his eyes still there… between her legs, which were spread wide. "Who knew pink and red could look so fucking good together?" There was awe in his voice.

"You're making it sound like you've never been with a redhead before."

"Only two percent of the population, Alabama. You're a rare and spectacular find."

"You already called me that this evening."

His eyes were hooded and a touch hazy. Shale frowned. "Alabama." He gave her a half-smile that had heat pooling in her belly. "You'll excuse me for the oversight, my mind is a little muddled right now. I can't promise it won't happen again."

Funny! She was kind of hoping he'd get it right. That he'd call her by her name, even if he didn't know he was doing it.

Then he was leaning in and licking on her clit like it was the tastiest little treat he had ever savored, and all rational thought fled her mind. All the air left both her lungs and the room, making it hard to breathe.

Georgia moaned. She groaned low and deep when he suckled on her clit. His head bobbed up and down, just a little.

Shale made this noise, like she was the best thing he had ever tasted. Then he laved on her some more, his golden eyes opening so that he could look at her.

Her mouth was open. Her breathing was ragged. Broken only by the odd moan or groan. She clutched on the sheets, trying to hold herself together. Trying not to let go too early. Truth was, she was so wound up. There was this tightening at the pit of her stomach. The need to come was quickly overtaking her.

He threw her a wicked grin before suckling on her clit again. One finger breached her opening. Just one. He worked it in and out of her a couple of times. His mouth felt so amazing... so... Georgia gave a quick punchy yell as she flew over the edge in a rush of ecstasy. Her head fell back as she moaned loudly. When she finally opened her eyes, one hand was buried in his hair and one of her legs was hooked around his shoulder.

"Glad you enjoyed that, Florida," he said as he licked his lips.

Shale had this pinched look. He almost looked angry. He gently took her leg off of him and rose up to his knees, his eyes raking over her. Georgia looked down. Her skin was flushed. She looked back up just as Shale gripped his cock in his hand. He fisted himself from base to tip. That had to be the sexiest thing she had ever seen. Ever!

A rush of need moved through her, so acute she almost groaned. It was like her orgasm from a few seconds ago had never happened.

"I'm going to turn you over now, California. I'm putting you onto all fours. I want you from behind." His voice was gravelly. "Are you okay with that?"

"Yes." A moan. Was she ever!

"I don't know you that well… yet. It'll be easier to find your g-spot that way."

Oh, god!

Had she died?

Was she in heaven?

He flipped her over. "Fuck!" he snarled. "Your ass is amazing."

She giggled at the awe in his voice. He really was that attracted to her. She glanced at him from over her shoulder while moving up onto all fours.

Shale's throat worked. His jaw was tense. His abs were popping. As were the muscles on either side of his neck. Wow! He was staring at her. All out staring.

He palmed her ass. "Fucking stunning. I knew you would be." Shale squeezed her globes. Heck, he all out worshipped her ass.

Shale crouched over her. She could feel his thick cock against her butt.

"Wait. What about protection?" How the hell had she almost forgotten?

CHAPTER 10

"*O*h shit! Of course. I almost forgot." *Her sentiment exactly.*

"*You do have a condom, I hope?*" *As much as she wanted him, she couldn't have a baby. No way. No condom. No sex!*

"Hold that position, Indiana. I'll be back in half a sec." He got off the bed and she watched him pick up his jeans, pulling a string of condoms out of his pocket. The guy had been out looking for a good time. This was evidence of that.

It was a good thing though. A bit of uncomplicated fun! All good!

The bed dipped as he climbed back onto it. She could hear him ripping at the foil. Shale made this little noise that told her he was putting on the condom. "You ready?" His voice was deep.

She wanted this so badly. "Yes, I am." *He sucked in a deep breath and pulled away from her.* "*I'm sorry I made you wait,*

Mississippi. I need you good and ready before…" His hot mouth closed over her… down there. Again! Holy shit! Again!

Georgia cried out. Her fingers dug into the duvet and she tried to pull away. Shale's hands held her hips so that she couldn't move. He dragged her down and onto his face. His tongue dipped into her opening. Shale licked her clit and then tugged on the small bundle of nerves with his teeth before licking her some more.

Shit!

Holy fuck!

She'd never had oral sex twice in a row and never in this position.

"Not sure… if you noticed…" He spoke against her clit. It felt good. His tongue kept licking between words. She was making really strange, strangled sounding noises and rocking her hips against his mouth. She couldn't make herself stop. The sensations were too intense. Her need too great. Oh, god! Without the bed holding her in place, she was pretty much fucking his face. "But I'm… pretty big." He tugged on her clit again. That baby was back to being mighty sensitive. "Need you good… and ready."

She was about to come… again. "Wait. Stop," she moaned. It was the hardest thing she had ever had to do, especially considering how close she was.

"Are you okay? Did I do something wrong?"

Georgia looked down, his mouth was shiny with her juices. He had the most intense expression. He really seemed to care about her feelings.

"I want you inside me and right now," she blurted before she changed her mind. Thing was, she had been skeptical about coming a second time in a row. There would be no chance of it happening during sex if he made her come again. She didn't orgasm as easily during the act. No more oral sex for her. Forget about it! She had this feeling that an orgasm with Shale inside her would be amazing. It was what she wanted right then. No! It was what she needed.

Shale licked his lips. Licked them clean with that long, talented tongue of his. His gaze went from blazing to inferno. He slipped out from under her. She felt Shale crouch over her. He was so big and warm. His dick throbbed against her ass. "You want me inside you?" he whispered against her ear.

"Yes." A whispered plea.

"I won't hurt you in any way, but I will be fucking you hard." His voice was a low growl.

Oh, god. She made a noise of agreement. Not quite trusting her voice.

She should be afraid. He was big and thick. She wasn't even a tiny bit scared. Her heart all but beat out of her chest in pure excitement.

Shale nuzzled into the back of her neck. "I might bite you, but don't try to pull away."

"Bite me?" What the hell? "Not too hard I hope."

He had to chuckle. "No, not too hard. I think you'll like it. I just don't want you to get a fright."

"O-okay." It turned her on. Was there something wrong with her? Biting was pretty kinky, wasn't it? It didn't matter, she was fully on board. As long as he didn't try to take a chunk out of her.

He sucked her earlobe and she bit down on her lower lip. "It'll feel good," he whispered. "All of it. I promise. Do you trust me, Wisconsin?"

She grinned. "Not really. I don't even know you." Her voice was a tad shrill.

"Then you're going to have to take a leap of faith here."

Georgia didn't doubt that it would feel good. Not for one second. "I'm good with that."

She felt him exhale in what seemed like relief. "One last thing," he added. "I might pin you down just before you come. That, and I will make a lot of noises during sex. I'm loud. I don't hold back."

"Let's go back to the pinning me down part." This needed to be discussed. "Pin me down?" she repeated. This time with a frown on her face to match the tone of her voice. She turned back to look at him.

"Yeah. I might hold you down so that you can't move. Not an inch. Don't panic or fight me, please. It's hard to explain. I'm just so turned on right now. Just ride it out if it happens. It's just that if I pin you, I'll bite you and then you'll come harder than you ever have before. That much I can promise you."

She laughed. It had a hysterical edge. "Why would you do that? Hold me down so I can't move." It sounded both interesting and fucking insane and all at once. Part of her was turned on and part of her was repulsed. Was he some kind of weirdo?

"I haven't had sex in a very long fucking time. I'm feeling on edge. I have a feeling your pussy is going to be tight and hot, like a slice of fucking heaven. Being inside you is going to turn me into a savage."

"Holy crap." His words turned her on. They shouldn't, but they did. Maybe she was more of a weirdo than she had thought.

"I'll find your sweet spot and then I'll hold you in place until you come… hard." One of his fingers found her clit. "Are you game or shall I finish licking you out?" He began rubbing on it. Softly, ever so softly. Her mouth opened up as she bit back a moan. "I just want you to know what you're in for before this goes down."

Shale pushed down on her clit with a single finger and nudged her opening with the tip of his cock. Not enough to breach her, but enough to create a need so fundamental, so all-consuming that she moaned. A pained noise. She felt wet trickle down the side of her leg.

"Even tighter than I thought." His voice was choked. "I have a feeling I might never want to leave." He pushed on her clit a second time and she gasped. His finger remained firm and steady against that little bundle of nerves, which seemed to throb in response, *repeatedly.*

Holy shit!

Holy crap!

Holy hell!

The pressure was arousing. It had all of her nerves flaring, her channel crying out, and she tried to push herself onto him. "I'm game…" She sounded breathless and needy.

Shale planted a kiss between her shoulder blades, another on her shoulder. His tongue traced the curve of her neck. "Once I start, I won't be able to stop until you come. Do you understand that?"

"Yes." It turned long and drawn out as he nudged into her. Her eyes widened up a whole lot and her mouth rounded into an O.

Shit!

Shit!

Shit*!*

It felt amazing already.

"Fuck," Shale groaned. "So good. Fuck!" A garbled, growly mumble.

Her breath was coming in sharp pants and her eyes were rolling back. Her pussy stretched tight and he slid in some more. Her mouth was open as she sucked in air. She couldn't seem to get enough of the stuff.

It took a few more careful thrusts before he was fully seated inside her. Right then she was so thankful she was soaking wet. Shale kept moving. His hips rocked gently, his dick barely moving, but he touched things in her she never knew existed. She was trying not to moan, but it felt so darned good.

"Are you ready?" A throaty rasp.

She groaned. Unable to speak for a moment. "Yes." High-pitched and needy.

Shale wrapped his hand around her hair, gripping a good chunk of it in his fist. He tugged her head back just a little. "Don't be afraid, please. I'm going to fuck you now." He pulled all the way out and then plowed into her. He held her in place with his hand on her hip and with the grip on her hair. It didn't hurt. His cock rammed back in... hard. His strokes were as graceful as they were forceful. She moaned. They were as punchy as they were deep.

Then he changed his angle and she cried out. What the...? *The sex gods must be smiling down on her or something because holy, freaking hell. She ground her teeth together to stop the noises that erupted from her. They were altogether too loud and crazy sounding.*

"Love your pussy," he growled as he pushed her onto the bed. Her face was to the side so she could still breathe, but she couldn't move. He'd been right about that. His body pinned her down. His cocked rammed into her. His hand tightened in her hair. It didn't hurt, but if he pulled any harder it would. If he held her any tighter, she would be damned sore.

It scared her, but it excited her. What was wrong with her? This was kinky, but it was so damned good. She had to work hard not to cry out, as in, loud.

There was nothing soft or careful about the way he took her. It was possessive and caveman. It was indeed savage. Panic rose up in her, even though there was pleasure, lots of it, since he hit her g-spot with every assault of his cock. Hard and fast. This was fucking. Pure and simple. Fucking at its most basic, its most carnal. Lord help her, but it was good. So very good.

He took her like more of an animal, making loud grunting noises with each hard thrust. Even that was a turn on. He sounded like a wild creature. Her chest was pushed up against the sheets. Her boobs pushed flat, her nipples so hard and sensitive against the cotton. She bit down on her lip, trying not to make too much noise. She failed hard, they both did.

Georgia tried to move and he growled... make that, he snarled.

A feral sound that had her heart racing. He sounded like a beast. His cock pounded in and out of her. It almost hurt. Almost. The pleasure was blinding. She'd never felt anything like it. Georgia couldn't move. Just like he promised. Not an inch. It only made her feel so much more. It was intense. There was a light sting on her head where he held her by the hair. That too heightened her senses.

One more hard thrust and she could feel everything in her tighten despite the panic at being held down and fucked so brutally. She could feel the air pulling into her lungs. He'd asked her to trust him and she would, even though he could snap her like a twig. Even though she was completely at his mercy.

He picked up the pace, his hips hitting her ass, his fingers digging into her flesh. His balls thudding against her. "Georgia! Oh, my fuck, Georgia," *he growled, his words almost incomprehensible.*

As he said her name for the second time, she felt everything in her release and all at once. There was a pinching sensation on her neck. It hurt. It also felt really good. Her orgasm went from fantastic to I'm-about-to-die amazing. Her heart even stuttered for a moment and considered giving up. Then it almost beat right out of her chest. Her eyes were wide in her head, her hands twisted in the sheets.

Shale's movements turned jerky and he roared. Loudly. It was insane. It was pure. She'd never felt more alive than right then.

His thrusts increased in tempo a whole hell of a lot before slowing. She could hardly catch her breath. Her body was vibrating. She moaned a little with every exhale. Her body felt like jello. He had been right about that. Like every bone in her body had been removed.

"Are you okay?" *Shale rubbed a hand down her back. She realized he was crouched over her, keeping his weight off her with his arms on either side of her.*

"Wow," *she croaked. Her throat hurt.* "That was… That…"

"Good? Painful?" *He sounded a bit panicked as he pulled away slightly, still inside her.* "I was far too rough. Fuck, I…"

"I'm fine. I…" She rolled her eyes. "I've never come that hard. You were right about the…" She felt her cheeks heat as she realized she had indeed screamed. She'd actually liked it when he'd bitten her. What the hell? *"About all of it," she mumbled.*

"Thank god!" She could hear he was smiling. "I was still too rough. It's been a while since I was with a hu—with someone. That's all! I lost my mind there for a moment or two. I swear I'll be more careful during round two."

"Round… Sorry?" Say what? Had she heard correctly?

"You heard me." He pulled away. "Oh no! Shit!" Shale said, sounding worried. He cursed again, louder this time. Then he inhaled through his nose.

She felt heat drip between her legs. "What is it?" Georgia sat up as well. She was far too wet down there. When she looked at him, she saw him tug on the condom, which was torn.

"Oh god!" She covered her mouth with her hand. "Oh no!" She squeezed her eyes shut. "It's okay." His voice held a soothing edge. "I had a medical just the other day." She watched his eyes lift in thought. "About three or four weeks ago. It was clear. I don't fuck around as much as you think. You won't get anything from me, I swear."

She believed him. Why, she couldn't say, but she did. "That's good to know. I don't want a baby." Georgia shook her head. "I can't be a mother right now. I just…" She had too much going on. Too many bills. Her mom needed her too much. Her credit card needed a credit card. She couldn't tell him any of that. "I have too many responsibilities as it is."

"I asked you to trust me before and you did. I need you to trust me now." He sucked in another breath through his nose. "You won't get pregnant by me."

How the heck would he know that? *"You can't be sure of that. It's impossible to know such a thing."* Unless…

"I swear to god, you won't become pregnant." He shook his head. "If you want, we can get dressed right now and find a drug store. If it will make you feel better, we can get you the morning after pill or..." He held up his hands. "We don't have to. If you're not comfortable with that, then..." He shrugged. "Shit! Hold on a sec." Shale stood up off the bed, his hand holding the condom onto his penis. He walked into a nearby room. Must have been a bathroom. He didn't bother with the light. She heard him rummaging around. The toilet flushing and water running, then he was striding back to her.

His cock was semi-erect still. He sat down on the bed next to her. "I can give you my number, if you want." He pushed out a breath. "But you won't get pregnant from me though. I swear to god, you won't." He looked so sure.

"You can't have kids, then?" It was silly, but Georgia felt sorry for him. That was the only way he could be so sure. "You're sterile?"

He pushed out a breath and nodded once, then looked down for a moment. "Like I said, you won't get pregnant. I'm happy to take whatever precaution you want. Happy to leave you with my number, but I'm not worried." He shook his head.

He looked completely relaxed.

"There won't be a drug store open at this time of night," she said, reaching for her bra, which was crumpled on the bed next to her. "Are you sad that you can't have kids?"

"Not in the least." He shook his head.

"Oh, okay, well, that's something at least. Hopefully, you don't change your mind about having kids. I think not being able to have children could be a hard thing to swallow. I'm sure you'll want to settle down... at some point."

Shale shrugged. "At some point, maybe. It's not something I've given too much thought to. I'm still young and..."

"Still having fun." She finished for him as she pulled her bra up, *tucking her boobs into the cups. "Listen to me going on and on. We weren't supposed to discuss anything personal, but I suppose a broken condom will change that."*

He nodded once before cocking his head and making a pained face. "I really wish you wouldn't do that." His eyes moved to her chest.

"Do what?" She raised her brows.

"I wish you wouldn't get dressed, Maine. There are still a couple of states left."

She was tempted. Very tempted but, unfortunately, the whole condom thing had taken the wind right out of her sails. "I think I should get home, before it gets too late." She glanced at her watch. There were a few minutes to go before midnight. Not too bad.

"It's early." Shale leaned over and kissed her shoulder. "There are still a couple of orgasms with your name on them."

"Only, you don't know my name." She laughed as she scooted off the bed, quickly retrieving her jeans.

"Fair enough." He leaned back on the bed. Georgia noticed that his cock was, once again, fully erect. The string of condoms lay on the bed next to him, the silver foil glinting. Taunting her.

Man oh man, but she was tempted. "In another life, I would have stayed." She did up the buttons on her jeans.

"I think you should stay now, since we only get one life." Shale folded his hands behind his head, looking hotter than hell during a volcano eruption.

She forced herself to look away and to find her top. "So, you're sure about the whole 'me not getting pregnant' thing?"

"One hundred percent sure, but," he jumped off the bed and rummaged through his jeans pulling out a hundred-dollar bill, "maybe you should take this in case you decide to——"

"No!" She held up her hand. "I don't want your money."

"I don't mean anything by…"

"*I know.*" *She forced herself to take in a deep breath.* "*I know how you meant it. I know you're just trying to do the right thing. I'll take care of it though.*" *She wasn't sure what she was going to do. How much did those pills cost? One thing was for sure, she wasn't taking his cash. She couldn't do it.*

Georgia pulled her head through her top. Shale was leaning over the desk in the corner. He looked like he was writing.

His ass was a thing of beauty.

Holy crap!! *Georgia had to force herself to look away. To pick her jaw up off the floor.*

"*Here.*" *Shale held a piece of paper in his hand with something scrawled on it.* "*Take this.*"

She began to reach for the page.

"*It's my number,*" *he added.*

She pulled her hand back. "*It's fine. I don't need it.*" *The guy was obviously telling the truth if he was willing to give her his number after such a quick hook-up. He'd said he didn't want kids. Shale wouldn't be this willing to stay in touch if he was lying.* "*You said I can't get pregnant, so, I'll take your word for it. I mean, why lie about something like that, right?*"

Shale nodded, looking serious. "*Right.*" *He picked up his jeans and tugged them on, leaving them undone.*

Good god! *'Eye candy' was an understatement. He was candy for her whole entire body. Not just her eyes.*

Enough of that! *This was serious. Georgia would go and check on the price of that pill in the morning versus what was left in her bank account – which wasn't much. She would weigh up the risk and make a decision then.* "*Thank you for—*" *She was stepping back towards the door when he put his arm around her and pulled her against him. Flush. She had to crane her neck to maintain eye contact.*

Shale smiled. "*No, thank you. I'm sorry that stupid condom ruined things."*

"It didn't. I had a good time." She smiled back.

"All I can say is that I hope I got your name right at least once..." He looked up in thought, a playful expression on his face. "Aaahhhhh..." He chewed on his full lower lip. "Maryland... Mary?" He raised his brows in expectation.

She laughed and shook her head.

"Okay." He shrugged his massive shoulders. "Well, you can't say I didn't try. Can I give you a ride?" He went to pick up his keys from the table.

"No! Please don't worry." She sounded a little forceful.

Shale turned back towards her, a frown on his face.

"I appreciate the offer," softer this time, "but I'll manage."

"You sure?" His frown deepened.

"Very." She pulled her phone out of her purse and within a few presses of the buttons she smiled at Shale. "There, an Uber will be here in two minutes. I'd better get going." She pointed at the door.

"Before you do." He closed the distance between them and kissed her. Softly. Carefully. Sweetly. "You take good care of yourself," he rumbled as he pulled back. "You are incredibly beautiful, don't let anyone try to convince you otherwise."

His words touched her, simply because he didn't need to say them. There was no other reason other than he meant them. "Thank you." She leaned up and touched her lips to his one last time before leaving. She felt a pang as she walked down the hallway. Stupid but hey, you couldn't help how you felt. Georgia wasn't a hook-up kind of a person. Shale was the opposite of any guy she had dated but... she felt something for him. Something more than lust? It didn't matter, because this was the last time she would see him.

CHAPTER 11

The last time. Yeah, right! It turned out he wasn't sterile. Georgia still hadn't been able to figure out how he could have ever been so sure she wouldn't become pregnant. The funny thing was that she still believed he had meant it when he said that to her. It didn't make any sense.

The oversized sweater she wore pulled tight over her bump. It rode up in the front, so she had to keep pulling the thing down. The crazy thing was that this was one of the best outfits she had. It was a green V-neck. The green accentuated her hair and her eyes, and the V helped in the boob department. They didn't look as big as they did in some of the other items of clothing she owned. Most things just plain didn't fit. Either her belly was too big, or her breasts were. Most times, however, she was too big in both departments.

Georgia wasn't sure how she was going to cope for too

much longer without proper maternity wear. The Joyces were insisting on paying for everything going forward, and she might just have to take them up on their offer.

Then there was Shale.

Did he really mean it about wanting to be this baby's father? Did he mean it when he said he wanted them to raise the child? She found that hard to believe, and yet her heart beat faster anyway. It was that illogical part of her making her feel this way. The part that was daring to hope. She hated and loved that part of her. She wanted it to be true. For the first time since becoming pregnant, she dared to dream about becoming a mom. She had thoughts of holding this baby in her arms, of rocking him or her. Georgia didn't allow herself to dwell on these thoughts. She couldn't. Not yet. Maybe not ever.

Her car door clicked shut and she put her keys in her purse, making her way to the little corner bakery. She could already smell something delicious baking inside. Probably cookies or cakes. The ones with lemon cream icing. *Yum!* Her mouth watered. She had enough cash on her for an herbal tea and that was it. There was food at home, nothing that would be this good, but she didn't need baked goods. Couldn't afford them, in more ways than one.

She was ten minutes early but hadn't been able to wait any longer. It wasn't like she could do any work since her brain was driving her nuts. It wouldn't shut up. It kept running through the events of their night together and then their brief meeting yesterday. Every word that was said. Every gesture. Everything. She was overanalyzing the lot.

Georgia pulled down on her sweater as she entered the

bakery come coffee shop. Her breath left her as Shale stood up from behind one of the two-man tables.

He looked even better in a white t-shirt and black jeans. His jaw was stubbled. His eyes were on her. He smiled, his jaw tight. Then he walked around the small table, pulling out a chair.

"Hi," he said as she drew nearer. "How are you... Alabama?" Shale frowned. "It occurred to me last night that I still don't know your name."

"Alabama is close enough." She sat down, pulling her chair in.

Shale sat down across from her. "I'm the father... of..." He glanced at her belly. "I'm the dad and you still won't even tell me your name." He was still smiling. Not as tense.

"Let's see how this goes and then maybe." He still had some answering to do. "Let's start with the whole 'sterile' thing. You led me to believe that you couldn't have kids. How else could you have been so sure that I wouldn't become pregnant?"

"Let's get you some tea. What kind do you prefer?"

"Just answer the question? It's not that hard. You had me convinced I wouldn't get pregnant. That it would never happen. I believed you. So much so that I didn't get that morning after pill. Stupid! I'm so stupid." She felt a pang of guilt immediately after saying it. Like she was wishing her baby away. This child was not to blame. This child was innocent in every way and deserved everything and more.

She grit her teeth for a moment, trying to gain composure.

"I'll get you some tea," Shale said, sounding concerned.

He pushed the chair back and headed for the counter.

What was he hiding? He *was* hiding something. That much was clear to her. It took him a few minutes to return and when he did, he not only had a mug with a teabag hanging over the edge, but he also had a plate full of tasty goodies.

"I wasn't sure what you liked," he put the plate down closer to her, "so I got us a couple of things."

"Donuts, a chocolate chip cookie, a blueberry muffin, cream puffs, a slice of pie… it's cherry." Shale handed her a fork and she took it.

Her mouth watered.

He slid the plate closer to her, taking one of the donuts off the plate, and taking a big bite. He groaned around the food. "That's so good." He licked the frosting off his lips, taking another bite. He gestured to the plate in front of her. "Not hungry, Wisconsin?"

"Don't." She shook her head. "This is no time for joking. It's serious. We need to talk about this."

"I *am* serious. I'm very serious. I'm here and I'm not going anywhere." He put what was left of the donut down on the plate and wiped his hands together. "Let's get out of here. Somewhere we can talk… somewhere a little more private." He looked around the room before turning his gaze back to her.

Georgia found herself glancing to the left and right of them as well. Aside from the lady working behind the counter, there was one other couple in the place, and a businessman in the far corner. The couple were in deep conversation with one another and the businessman was reading a newspaper while enjoying a Danish. The server was too busy frosting cupcakes behind the counter, to pay them much attention. "No one cares what we're talking about. No one is paying any attention to us. I get the distinct impression that you're either trying to buy time or that you're hiding something."

"It's not what you think." He grimaced.

"I don't think anything. I have no idea what to think and it's driving me a little nuts." *Unless...* "Have you changed your mind? About this? About the baby?" That was most likely it. He was too afraid to say so in case she made a scene.

"No," he answered immediately. "It's just, you might have a hard time dealing with what I have to say. It might—"

Oh shit! "You're married." She squeezed her eyes shut and rubbed a hand over her face. "You already have a couple of kids and—"

"What?" He frowned. "No! That's not it at all." He frowned some more.

"Tell me then. Just spit it out." When he didn't anything she went on. "Just tell me. I can take it."

"It's not that simple. Trust me on that one."

What else could it be? What was so bad? What was he skirting around? "You're moving to Iceland? You just lost your job and need to move in with me." That was probably it. Then again, she could think of worse. "Your family has some kind of genetic disorder and you're afraid the baby might be affected?"

He choked out a laugh but quickly sobered. "You have some imagination there, Indiana." Then he raised his brows in thought for a moment. "Although you're not far off."

"On which guess? You can't move in with me. I'm sorry, but—"

"That's not it. I… are you sure you don't want to take a walk? I'd prefer—"

"Tell me, Shale, before I lose my shit. It won't look pretty, I can tell you that much. I'm far too pregnant to be losing my shit—"

"I'm a shifter."

Georgia could not have heard right. "What's that?"

"The thing about the genetics. It's kind of true since I'm…" he looked around them and even leaned forward on the table, "I'm a shifter." He kept his voice down. "Not one of the regular kind either."

"A shifter?"

"Keep your voice down." His eyes darted to the couple and then to the lady behind the counter.

Georgia picked her jaw up off the floor and took a big gulp of her tea. Thankfully it had cooled down or she would have burned herself. "A shifter but not the regular kind?" She realized she was repeating what he was saying but couldn't seem to stop herself.

He pushed out a breath, running a hand through his hair. "Yep, I'm a… shifter."

She was sure she heard him whisper the word 'dragon.'

"Okay, so I know shifters exist, although I've never met one." Her voice was a bit shrill.

"Um… yes, you have. That's what I'm trying to tell you here. All of the guys I was with, we're all…" He widened his eyes.

"Dragon shifters," she whispered.

Shale smiled and nodded. "Yes, exactly. We live in a vast territory to the north. That doesn't matter right now. We don't live amongst humans, although we mix with you guys from time to time and have been taking human mates."

He sounded so believable. Like he meant every word. Like he *believed* every word.

"I'm a prince in my tribe." He leaned even closer to her, pulling his shirt down a little and revealing what looked like a tattoo on his chest. It was pretty elaborate. A golden tribal type of artwork with dark swirls. His chest was still broad and muscular and—She needed to stop with that particular line of thought.

"That's one hell of a tattoo," Georgia found herself saying, despite the crazy stuff coming out of his mouth. "Did you have it done in the last six months?"

"It's not a tattoo," he corrected her, shaking his head. "That's what I'm trying to tell you. I was born like this. All dragon shifters have these markings."

"Oh!" *Yeah, right!* "Why didn't you have it on you that night?"

"I did. We wear a special concealer. It would be odd if all of us had similar golden or silver chest markings. The hunters know of these markings." He touched his chest. "If they were to catch wind of our activities on human soil, they would devise plans to capture us."

Shale was completely certifiable. It was worse than she could ever imagine. "Oh, o-okay." Georgia wasn't sure what else to say.

"I didn't think you would become pregnant because you weren't anywhere close to your heat. We have much better-developed senses. I'm not sure what happened there." He shrugged. "I guess it's not an exact science." He took a sip of his soda. "Normally we can scent if a female is nearing her heat, and you weren't. At least, that's what I thought." He shrugged.

Or maybe it was because he didn't have heightened senses. He only believed he had them. She felt so bad for Shale. Georgia understood mental illness to some degree. She was watching dementia steal her mother from her one day at a time. It was horrible.

"You're taking this better than I expected." Shale smiled again. He looked so normal. So darned believable.

Georgia took another sip of her tea, holding her belly with her other hand. *Oh, baby, I'm so sorry.*

"This next part might scare you." He took a sip of his soda.

As if everything he had just said hadn't scared the bejesus out of her.

When she didn't say anything, he went on. "You're carrying twins…" he grimaced expecting a reaction out of her, when he didn't get one, he carried on, "and you are going to have them any day now. Like I said," he glanced at the couple, before locking eyes with her, "we have taken human mates who have had our offspring. Our females only carry for six months. It's very rare for a female to have more than two. Twins are the norm." He smiled again. "I really thought you were going to freak out." He looked relieved, even sitting back in his chair for a moment or two before leaning forward again. "We're having boys. So far, no human has birthed a girl, so chances are good we will have sons."

She took another sip of her tea, not tasting anything. Georgia nodded once. *What the hell was she going to do?*

"…and they're dragon shifters. They'll even have a mark on their chests, only, chances are good it won't be golden like mine. You see I've undergone allergy treatment for our aversion to silver so…" He chuckled.

"I'm bombarding you with information. Too much too soon, yes?"

"You could say that." She nodded again.

How was she going to tackle this? She couldn't just leave him there. He was in the middle of a major breakdown or episode or something. "So…" she smiled, "do you perhaps have a family member who we can call to join us? Your mom or dad maybe?" She tried to sound light and breezy. "I would love to meet your family."

"Um…" he looked confused, cocking his head, "both my parents are… they're staying on our dragon lands, nowhere near our main settlement."

"Oh, I see." *Shit!* "Any other family?" *Act normal!* She forced out a smile.

"I have a sister and several brothers, including a twin."

"I see." She nodded. "Let's call him if—"

"No one is available right now and," he scratched the back of his head, "there will be plenty of time for that soon enough." He cocked his head looking confused.

She needed to do something more drastic. "Did you take your medication this morning?"

Shale made a face of complete confusion, his forehead furrowed. Then he looked taken aback. "What medication would that be? I…" Then he fell back in his chair. "You don't believe a word I've just said, do you? That's why you're taking this so well?"

She pushed out a breath. "Shale, I'm just trying to help you. I know that's difficult to understand. Have you been seeing someone? A psychologist?"

"Of course not! There is nothing wrong with me, Virginia… Indiana… Wyoming…"

Shit! He was getting agitated.

"I wish I knew your name." He pushed a hand through his hair, mussing it a little. The couple from the table next to them had stopped talking. They were listening in. "You do know…" He glanced at the couple, giving them a dirty look. His jaw clenched and his eyes got an aggressive look.

"Honey," the guy at the table said, his voice a touch high-pitched – especially for a man, "um… I think we should go now." His eyes stayed on Shale the whole time.

"Yes." His partner's eyes were wide and filled with fear. They were also trained on Shale. She pushed her chair back. "I think that might be a good idea."

Shale waited until they were gone, only then did he relax just a little. Perhaps 'relaxed' was the wrong word. It was more a case of not being as agitated than actually being relaxed.

"I am who I say I am. You do know that shifters exist? If not, you're living under a rock. There are several non-human species."

"Yes, I know." It was true. "But I've never heard of dragons. There is no such thing."

"Look at me…" He clenched his jaw in frustration, probably because he didn't know her name. She should have told him by now but… she couldn't. Not now. Especially not now. "I mean really look at me." He gestured down his torso. "Do I look human to you?"

"Yes."

"Look closer."

"You're big." She looked him up and down. "Not just big, but really tall as well. Bigger than most guys but that's not proof of—"

Just then a group of three giggling teenagers walked in and jostled their way to the counter.

"I would like nothing more than to prove it to you, but… I can't right now." Shale spoke under his breath. "I'm telling you the absolute truth. Let's go somewhere and I'll…"

"I can't." *Like hell!* She shook her head. "I need to get back to work."

"I'm serious. You are going to have these babies any day." He stood up as well, walking to her.

Georgia had to work hard not to take a step back. Her heart beat really fast. She could hear it in her ears. *Thump… whoosh! Thump… whoosh! Thump… whoosh!* Shale was dangerous. Or maybe he wasn't. Truth was, she couldn't be sure right then. She had the baby to think of. "We can meet in a couple of days."

"I have a feeling that when you walk out that door, it's going to be the last time I see you." He was clenching his jaw again. His eyes were intense.

"That's not true."

"Like hell." He spoke under his breath, which was almost worse than if he had been screaming. "You think I'm crazy."

"I think you might need help, but I—"

"There you go! Admit that when you leave it's over."

"You are still this baby's father, even if you do need help. Shale, please, you are scaring me."

He sniffed the air. His whole demeanor softened. "Shit! I'm sorry. I didn't mean—"

"It's okay. I won't just leave and cut ties. I would never do that."

He pushed out a breath. "Please…" He glanced at the young girls who were openly admiring him. They giggled as he looked their way. "Shit!" he said under his breath. "I can prove it to you if you'll just trust me, please."

She wanted to. She burned to, but she couldn't. There was just no way. It was too far-fetched. A dragon? A prince? Twins? No way! Just no way! "I can't." She stepped back, getting ready to run if she had to and—

There was a popping sound. An honest-to-god popping sound. Water gushed down from between her legs. Georgia's first thought was that she had wet her pants. That all of this stress had caused her to lose control of her bladder. Then she realized what it was.

CHAPTER 12

"Oh, no!" Her face morphed into one of utter shock. Shale watched as the blood drained from her features. "My water just broke. Oh…" She put a hand to her belly. "Ohhh!" She clenched her teeth. "I think… I think I'm having a contraction. No! Oh no! It's too early."

"That's what I've been telling you. It's not too early. This is happening right on time. The babies are fine."

"Stop with the—" She groaned, her face pinched, her eyes closed.

He gripped her elbow. "Everything is going to be ok. Please tell me your name already," Shale urged.

Her eyes were wide, and she was doing this weird breathing thing. There was no way she was talking right then. "Let's go outside." He tried to take her arm, but she pulled away, still breathing heavily.

"Do you want me to call an ambulance?" the female behind the counter asked. The group of young females looked both fascinated and horrified.

"No!" he growled.

The server flinched at his harsh tone.

"No ambulance," he added, softer this time.

"Yes!" Alabama – or whatever the hell her name was – nodded, eyes on the server.

"Hold on just a second," he asked the server, who had just picked up her phone. She looked seriously spooked.

"I can get you help," he tried again, gripping her elbow carefully. "Please just tell me your name. Let's start there."

"Georgia. It's Georgia."

Shale sighed. He couldn't help the smile that formed on his lips. "Good to finally officially meet you."

Georgia made a pained face, this time not from actual pain. "Why do you have to sound so normal?"

"Because I am normal, New York. I'm completely fine. I swear to god. Let me help you. My SUV—"

Georgia shook her head, eyes still wide. Both hands on her belly. "Call them!" she yelled, looking over at the server.

"I can help," he insisted. "Get in my car. I can drive us somewhere secluded," he spoke quickly and softly and directly into her ear. "I'll shift into my dragon form and fly you back to my lair. There are healers there who can help you," he continued. Shale realized how unbelievable this sounded but he had to try. "You are going to have dragon whelps… don't get me wrong, they'll look human—"

"Of course they will. '*They.*' Listen to me," she muttered to herself. "My baby will be normal," she pushed out. "Because he or she *is* human." She moaned, arching her back a little. "I'm having another one. Oh god… it's bad."

"Maybe you should sit." The server pushed over a chair.

Why hadn't he thought of that? He helped Georgia to the chair and helped her sit.

The female had a phone to her ear. "The nine-one-one operator says that help is on the way." She listened for a moment or two, nodding her head at whatever they were saying to her over the phone. "Okay… thank you. Yes, I will." Then she looked down at Georgia. "They are three minutes out," she said.

Georgia nodded once, grimacing. She was doing that breathing thing again. "Thank you," she groaned.

"Is there anything else I can do?" the female asked, looking concerned.

Georgia shook her head once.

"I've got this," Shale said. "I'll take care of my… girlfriend."

Georgia shot him a look that spoke volumes. She was still breathing through the birthing pains, so she didn't make any comment.

"I'm going to wait outside," the server said. "The ambulance will be here soon."

Shale went on his haunches in front of Georgia. He didn't have a clue of what to do. How did he prove to her that he wasn't off his rocker? He didn't want to freak her out by making his eyes slitted, or by making scales appear on his skin. Also, everyone in the place had their eyes on them. Someone might see. Chances were good that would happen. He couldn't take such a big risk. If only she'd agreed to meet back at her place. He could have partially shifted or something. Now the babies were coming, and she wanted nothing to do with him. Even worse, she believed he was crazy. He watched as she worked her way through the birth pain. Georgia finally slumped back in the chair.

"Can I get you a water?"

She shook her head. "I'm okay." She pointed to the floor. "You can hand me my purse."

He did as she asked. Georgia rummaged through her purse, pulling out her phone. She pushed a few buttons and put the phone to her ear. "Macy… I'm so glad you picked up." She spoke rapid-fire, her voice shrill. "I'm in labor."

Shale didn't mean to listen in, but he couldn't help it. "Riiiight! Tell me another one." Her friend giggled.

His gut twisted when he saw tears gathering in her eyes. "I mean it," Georgia sniffed. "I wouldn't joke about something like this. I'm waiting for the ambulance. My water broke." she sniffed again. "I'm so scared," she whispered.

"What? Oh, my god! Oh, no! Where are you? Are you at home? Shall I come over? What do you need me to do? I've suddenly gone completely blank."

"I'm not at home," Georgia answered.

Shale could hear sirens in the distance. They were drawing steadily closer.

"Where are you? Oh shit, are you alone? With your mom? Do you need me to come over right away?"

"There's an ambulance on its way and… I'm…" She frowned, looking at Shale. "I-I'm not alone." She sounded hesitant. Like being with him was worse than being all alone.

Macy pushed out a heavy sigh of relief. "Oh, thank

goodness. Who's with you?"

"Shale." Georgia smiled at him too brightly.

"Well, that's good, since he's the father."

"Is it?" Georgia spoke as if she was exceedingly happy. She had no idea he was listening in.

"Well, isn't it?" Shale could hear the question in her voice. "He should be there. Is everything okay? I mean, besides the obvious."

"Um… could be better. Please meet us at the hospital. I need you."

"Of course," Macy answered without hesitation. Shale liked the female. "I need five minutes to get dressed, and then I'm on my way."

"It's after lunchtime on a Sunday, you laz—" Georgia clutched her belly. She groaned. "It's another contraction. There're coming quite quickly." She groaned some more. "They're quite strong as well."

"Okay, I'll see you at Dalton Springs Hospital."

Georgia said a groaned yes and handed the phone to Shale. He pushed the end button and put the phone in her purse. By now the sirens were blaring. He figured the ambulance was on their street. She continued to breathe through her pains. "Can I rub your back?"

Georgia shook her head, groaning.

"You're doing a really great job." He rubbed the side of her arm, trying to be encouraging when all he felt was useless.

The door to the coffee shop burst open and two uniformed individuals appeared. They carried a stretcher. And one of them carried an oversized bag.

The server rushed in behind them, pointing at Georgia. "Make way for the paramedics!" she shouted. That's her…

over there!" She yelled unnecessarily, since the paramedics were already making their way over to them.

"Oh, thank god," Georgia half-yelled. Her cheeks were flushed. Her brow was sweaty. Her jeans were soaked through. "This feels like it's happening quickly. It shouldn't be happening this quickly."

"First-time mom?" the female paramedic asked.

Georgia nodded.

"First-time labor is rarely all that quick, but we won't waste any time getting you to the hospital just to be sure." The male winked at Georgia and Shale felt his hackles rise which was stupid given the situation. He knew that his instincts were kicking in. He was about to become a father. It was normal for a shifter to become possessive.

"Rick over here has delivered several babies in his career." The female gestured to her colleague.

"All true." Rick nodded.

"We're going to ask you to lie down on the stretcher," the female said.

Georgia nodded. She got up off the chair with Shale's help. The male, Rick, tried to move in. Shale growled low. A deep rumble. It just happened. He couldn't help it.

"Shale. Stop that!" Georgia said.

The paramedic took a step back. "Um… ah… who's the Pitbull?" he asked, eyes on Shale.

He wanted to growl again. Shale wanted to snarl at the male in warning but managed to hold it back. Georgia would really think he was crazy if he did that.

"Her boyfriend." Shale narrowed his eyes, helping Georgia onto the stretcher.

"No, he's not," Georgia snapped.

"I'm the father," Shale tried again.

Georgia didn't say anything.

"Would you mind taking a step back, please, so that I can do my job?" the male asked.

Shale clenched his jaw for a moment or two before doing as the paramedic asked. Rick was a healer after all. He seemed to know what he was doing. Shale didn't have to like it though. "Be careful with her," he grumbled.

They lifted Georgia and headed out. Shale followed closely behind them. Georgia moaned and clutched at her belly.

"Breathe, honey," the female paramedic urged.

They had her loaded in the back of the parked ambulance within a minute. Shale tried to get inside.

"I'm sorry, sir." The female shook her head. "No one may ride in the emergency vehicle but the patient. It's company policy." She gave him a small smile. "I promise this baby isn't coming for at least a couple of hours yet. You can follow us in your own car." She winked at him.

He was used to human females being nice to him. This female was no exception. "Fine," he said. It wasn't like he had much choice.

"We will take good care of your... of the mother of your child."

He nodded once in thanks.

"Hang in there." He spoke up so that Georgia would hear him. The male paramedic was putting an oxygen mask on her face. He was familiar with some of the human medical equipment after undergoing the allergy immunotherapy for his silver affliction.

He headed for the SUV at a run, careful not to go too fast and giving himself away. Only when his vehicle was behind the ambulance, did he calm by a hair.

Shale followed behind them, the sirens blared and flashed. The trip lasted all of a couple of minutes.

He parked in the first open bay he spotted and got out. Shale needed to be there when they took her out of the ambulance.

"Sorry, sir. Sorry… excuse me," a male in uniform approached, "you can't park here. It's one of the doctor's parking spots."

"It's an emergency," he growled, jogging to where they were taking Georgia from the ambulance.

"It always is," the male muttered to himself. "Your vehicle will be impounded!" he shouted after Shale who kept jogging.

Shale didn't give a shit. He really didn't. He could buy a half a dozen more of the same. He needed to be there for Georgia, even if she didn't want him. The shit was going to hit the fan at some point, and he had to be there to deal with the fallout. His whelps were coming. He was going to be a father. A lump formed in his throat.

"How are you doing?" he asked as he arrived at Georgia's side, they had just taken the stretcher out of the ambulance and were wheeling her to a large emergency entrance. He wanted to take her hand, but he didn't.

She was at the end of what looked like a particularly bad contraction. At least he could remember some of the stuff he Googled the night before. Her breathing was slowing though. Her brow was covered in a light sheen of sweat.

To hell with it!

Shale gripped her tiny hand in his, giving it a squeeze.

"This baby is coming," she spoke into the mask, misting it up. "My contractions are hectic." She looked fearful.

"They *are* quite close together," the female paramedic said; she had a tight smile on her face. "Your contractions are about three minutes apart."

Despite consulting Google, both last night and this morning, Shale wasn't sure what that meant. He had some idea of what they were talking about, but he couldn't remember exact details. Only that the birthing pains got stronger and more frequent as the time for pushing drew closer. *Was three minutes too quick?* "This is supposed to take eleven to sixteen hours on average." He felt panic well. He'd hoped to be able to give Georgia a sign. Show her somehow that he wasn't a mental case. He needed to get her out of there and back to the lair where it was safe.

The paramedic smiled at him. "It's not an exact science. Also, premature births tend to go quicker. Let's get you settled in a bed. The nurses will take you to your ward and then your doctor will be right in."

Georgia nodded, she pulled her mask off. "I need to get hold of the Joyces. You took my purse."

"No, you don't." He had her purse clasped in one hand.

They moved her onto a bed, counting down from three. "I do, Shale. They're—"

"No," he swallowed thickly, "these babies are ours. We'll raise them, we'll—"

"No!" she yelled. "Please. You need help. Call someone. A friend. One of your brothers."

"I don't need help. I'm here. I'm not going away. I won't let you give our children away. I meant everything I said. I'm not... I'm not crazy." Softer this time.

"Goodbye." The male paramedic waved. "All of the best."

"Good luck," the female said. "Take care." She winked at Shale.

"Thank you," Georgia said, before turning her eyes to him. "The Joyces are good people. They've agreed to cover my medical expenses. They'll give him or her a good life. I've told you all this already." She begged him with her eyes. "I want nothing more than to raise this child…" Her eyes welled with tears all over again and this time they spilled over. "The baby is going to need medical help and that costs money. Money I don't have right now." She grit her teeth as more tears fell. "It's far too early." She shook her head, wiping her eyes.

"*I'll* cover your medical expenses." He pulled out his wallet, taking out his credit card.

"That's sweet but… come on, Shale! You don't have any money and even if you did, I'm not taking it."

"Why not?" He kept walking next to the bed. They turned into a room.

"To the labor ward," one of the nurses announced. "Sir," she addressed him, "I'm going to need you to fill out some forms. We'll need patient information and your information as well, if you're going to cover the expenses. I overheard."

"He's not," Georgia said.

"I am," Shale said at the same time.

"Don't do this…" she began but another birthing pain was taking hold. Georgia began panting.

"I'll have the forms brought up to you," the female stated.

"Thank you," Shale said, jogging to catch up with Georgia, who was being wheeled to an elevator. He put a hand out and stopped it just before the doors closed.

The nursing staff were asking Georgia questions. What had happened? How long she had been in labor. Then her birthing pains started up again.

One of the females turned to him. "You're the husband, then?" she asked, smiling.

"Boyfriend. The baby is mine," he stated.

The elevator dinged to announce that they'd reached the right floor and Georgia was wheeled out. She clutched her stomach, panting her way through the pain.

Shale heard the footfalls of someone running and looked in that direction. It was Macy. She looked panicked. "Oh, my god!" she yelled. "Are you okay? Of course you're not okay. Oh, hun…" She took Georgia's hand.

"You need to stay." Georgia sounded panicky. She glanced Shale's way. Great, she was still scared shitless of him.

"I told you I would be there for you and here I am." Macy looked at him. "I'm glad you're here too." The female had no idea.

There were various kinds of equipment. Georgia was moved onto one of the beds, just as another pain kicked in.

"Give your wife this to wear." The healer handed him a green gown. "We'll be back in five minutes. Doctor should be here by then as well."

He nodded once. Macy was whispering words of encouragement to Georgia.

It didn't take long for the pain to subside. Georgia slumped back against the bed. He handed Macy the gown, since he had the distinct impression Georgia wouldn't want help from him. "Would you mind helping her put this on?"

He felt useless all over again. He pointed at the door with a bathroom sign on it. "I can leave as well, if you would prefer."

"No," Georgia shook her head. "It would be more private in there."

"Let me help you," he began.

Just then a female with a clipboard knocked once and walked in. The door to the ward was open. "Good afternoon. I'm Jessica, I have your paperwork here, sir." She handed the board to Shale, who took it. There was a pen attached. "I'd like to ask that you come through to reception on the ground floor once the paperwork has been completed. You will need to make a down payment."

"Wait! What?" Georgia asked, brows raised.

"A down payment is standard for patients covering their own medical expenses."

"What kind of a down payment are we talking about?" Georgia asked.

"It doesn't matter," Shale said.

Unfortunately, the female carried on. "It's ten thousand dollars for a standard vaginal birth. More, if complications are found."

Georgia clutched at her belly, her face turning redder as the pain took hold. "That's ridiculous. You can't possibly pay that, Shale. Let's call—"

"I can!" He nodded at the female who had brought the forms. "I'll be down shortly." He tapped the board. "After filling these out."

The female gave them a tight smile and left.

"You can't…" Georgia was panting and trying to talk.

"Of course he can," Macy cut in. "Shale is the father of this baby. Let him make the down payment already."

"I need to call the Joyces," Georgia insisted, between pants.

"No!" Shale yelled. There was no way he was allowing that couple to adopt his whelps.

"Let's all calm down," Macy interjected. "Let Shale cover the costs for now. Don't stress over that. We can always call the Joyces once we've seen the doctor."

"They wanted to be there for the birth," Georgia pushed out. "This baby is coming… it's coming," she repeated, her face crumpled in pain. Not just the physical kind.

"The Joyces will live." Shale managed to keep his voice even this time. "We're not giving our child away. It's not happening. Macy is right, we can talk about it." Once the babies came, she would know he wasn't full of shit.

Georgia groaned, she still held her belly. Her eyes were squeezed shut. Within ten seconds, the pains were easing. "I need to change." She got off the bed and Macy helped her from the room.

Shale began filling out the forms. He used a fake ID. He had no idea about most of the questions about Georgia. He knew next to nothing about the soon-to-be mother of his whelps. It was a daunting thought.

CHAPTER 13

"What are you doing?" Macy asked as soon as they were in the bathroom. "Why can't you accept money from the father of this baby? It's not a bad thing. It's not a handout. He's the father, for heaven's sake."

Her back was killing her. "He's not what you think." She pushed the heel of her hand to the base of her spine.

"Shale is here. As in, he's present and he's supportive. I think it's great that he wants to cover the costs. It seems like he's against this adoption." Macy looked her in the eyes. "I know you don't want to give this baby away." Her voice took on a tender edge. "You've tried to hide it, but I know. I can see it. I'm your best friend, remember?"

"I *don't* want to give this baby up, Macy," Georgia said as she pulled off her sweater, "of course I don't want to, but what choice do I have? None! I have my mom to think of. I have this baby to think of too. I can't do what I want. I have to do the best thing for everyone involved."

"Everyone but you, and that's not right. It seems to me that things have changed. You might have plenty of choices now that Shale's here."

"That's just it." She undid her bra. "I don't."

"That doesn't make sense." Macy handed her the gown and she pulled it over her head. "You need to give him a chance."

"He told me he's a shifter."

Macy's eyes widened. "No shit! He's a shifter?" She sounded flabbergasted and a tad excited.

"Keep your voice down," Georgia said. "I don't want them to admit him… just yet. I think he's harmless and so—"

"Admit him? What are you talking about?" She took on a puzzled look. "Oh! You don't believe him. Shifters exist, Georgia. He might be telling the truth. He could be one. You realize that, don't you? Shifters exist, and come to think of it, he *is* huge. His eyes are also… different. Those guys he was with were big too. Rock's eyes were a freaky ice-blue." Her friend's voice was animated. She spoke quickly, looking excited. "It could be true, that's all I'm saying."

"There's more. He says he's a *dragon* shifter. A prince. He lives in a…" *What was the word he had used?* "A lair." *Shit!* She could feel the muscles in her belly start to tighten. Georgia pulled down the toilet seat. It landed with a bang. Then she sat down, breathing as her stomach pulled tighter and tighter still. Like a vice around her middle. Like a terrible cramp. The ones that had a person holding back a scream and praying for a reprieve. She'd had a couple of them in her calf muscle before. Like that, only much worse, since it involved her entire mid-section.

"Are you okay?" Macy asked as she came back from the pain.

"Yeah." She nodded.

"That bad, huh? This whole 'giving birth' thing is not for the faint of heart."

"That's for sure." Georgia nodded., still trying to catch her breath. "Help me up, so that I can change."

Macy helped her to her feet. "You don't believe him, then?"

"He says he's a prince. That I'm pregnant with twins. That the babies aren't human. They will be boys and the gestation period for dragon offspring is six months, so they are being born full-term right now and will be absolutely fine." She lifted her eyes in thought, trying to recall all of the crazy things he had said. "He said they will have chest markings."

"Chest markings?"

"Yep, similar to tattoos, only not." Georgia removed her wet jeans and underwear.

"Okay, I'll admit, that does sound a bit on the wacky side." Macy made a face. "Okay, a lot on the wacko side."

"The guy lives in fantasy land."

Macy frowned. "He seems so normal. Normal and gorgeous… and cuckoo." She made a swirling motion with her finger at her temple.

"Good-looking people have mental illnesses as well," Georgia remarked. "Now you know why I can't accept money from him. He says he's mega-wealthy but that might be one of his crazy ideas. How can I possibly accept any kind of money from someone with mental issues? It could land him in serious crap."

"Don't stress about that now."

"I have to! I have to call the Joyces." The idea of being this baby's mom was... it was amazing. It left her feeling dizzy. It made tears gather in her eyes and had her heart swelling in her chest. "The fact of the matter is that this baby is coming and he or she is going to need a ton of medical care." A sob left her. Georgia put her hand over her mouth. Up until then, she'd done a good job of keeping it together, but it was getting more and more difficult with each contraction. "I can't believe I'm in labor. It's too early, Macy."

"Don't stress about any of it now. You need to focus on this baby. On staying calm and positive." Her friend took her hand. "Forget about the Joyces for now. Call them once the baby comes. They will live if they're not here. I can see that even the idea of calling them stresses you out, so don't do it."

"I was supposed to have more time to prepare mentally." A tear ran down her cheek. "I'm not ready to do this."

"The baby is coming, my friend."

"Not that... Okay, that too. I'm mainly talking about giving him or her up." She put a hand to her belly. "This is so hard."

"I'm here. I'm not going anywhere. Let's focus on the here and now."

Georgia nodded. "Thank you, and you're right." She nodded, wiping a couple more tears away. She was so afraid of what was going to happen. She was so worried for her baby.

Georgia needed to sit on the toilet for another contraction before making her way back to the bed.

Shale was talking with a doctor. At least, she looked like

a doctor. She had her long hair pulled up in a ponytail. She was holding a file and had a stethoscope around her neck. "You must be Georgia." She had a friendly face. "I'm your gynecologist, my name is Doctor Michaels."

She nodded. "Good to meet you."

"I need to ask a couple of questions. Your partner filled me in on what happened earlier," the doctor said. "You should lie down."

Georgia did as she said.

"How far along are you?" She held a pen in one hand and a clipboard in the other.

"I'm six months, almost to the day."

"How many weeks since your last check-up?" she asked.

Georgia felt her cheeks heat. They must be turning a bright red. She swallowed hard. "I haven't been for a check-up. I don't have health insurance."

"Before you say anything," there was a growl to Shale's voice, "I will be paying for the birth and whatever else is needed, in full."

"I wasn't going to say anything." The doctor smiled. "I understand that medical care can be very expensive."

"I would have gone but," she picked at the quick of one of her nails, "I guess I buried my head in the sand for a while there and… I just couldn't afford to. I should have though. It's no excuse." She should have faced up to reality sooner. Georgia never expected this to happen, though.

"You don't have to explain anything to me. Neither of you do." She looked from Shale back to her. "I'm here to ensure your and the baby's safety during this birth. I'm not here to judge in any way."

"Thank you." Georgia licked her lips, feeling relieved. Thing was, seeing a specialist, paying for a scan. Paying for everything herself. There was just no way. It would have been her food money for at least a week. It had taken her a while to acknowledge that she was going to have to give this baby up. "I was supposed to see someone this coming week but…" She let the sentence die. It didn't matter anymore.

Doctor Michaels smiled reassuringly. "Your membranes have ruptured but with drugs and antibiotics, we can try to suppress your contractions. We need to try to keep this baby inside you for at least twenty-four hours."

"What if it doesn't work?" Georgia sounded nervous. Her eyes were wide. Her hand caressed the curve of her belly.

"If you have this baby today, at six months gestation, the chances of survival nowadays are roughly ninety percent."

"So high?" Georgia pushed out a sigh of relief. "Still though, there is a chance that—"

"No." Shale said. "It won't happen! You don't have to worry." His voice held an edge of frustration. "Our child will be strong."

"You can't say that for sure," Georgia muttered. She let it go – it was no use arguing with Shale. She'd learned that the hard way with her mom.

"Look," the doctor interrupted, "we'll give you steroids to mature the baby's lungs. If we can slow this thing down or even stop it for a day or two, the odds go up exponentially. Then you have to pray for a girl." The doctor smiled, clearly joking. Obviously trying to lighten the mood. "Girls tend to develop faster than boys. Pink is gorgeous and, best of all, girls don't pee all over the place when you take off the diaper."

The whole thing only made Shale scowl deeply. His eyes even darkened slightly. "That's just it," he blurted. "We're having a boy child," he added when no one said anything.

"Oh." The doctor's smile broadened. "Typical guy." She laughed. "Hoping for a boy." She shook her head. "I'm only teasing about the whole girl thing anyway. It doesn't matter either way. Let's take this one step at a time. It doesn't help worrying and stressing."

Doctor Michaels pulled on a pair of rubber gloves with a snap. "I need to check how dilated you are. Your contractions may not go away completely but you may stop or slow down on dilating further for a while. I need to have a reference point. You can use the sheet to cover your lower end," she advised, and Macy helped her pull the sheet up to her hips. "Please bend your knees and open your legs for me," the doctor instructed.

Georgia did as she asked.

She used the sheet to shield her. "This might hurt a little. It will be uncomfortable, I'm afraid."

Georgia nodded. "That's fine."

The doctor applied what looked like lubricant to her fingers and leaned down between Georgia's legs.

Georgia made a squeaking noise as the doctor inserted her fingers into her vagina. She yelped as pain flared and then it was over. She couldn't help but notice that there was blood on the doctor's gloves as she pulled them off her hands, throwing them in a bin for contaminated materials. "You're already six centimeters dilated."

"What does that mean?" Georgia wracked her brain to try to remember the different stages of labor.

"Ten centimeters means that the baby is ready to be born?" Shale stated. "I read that last night."

"Correct." Doctor Michaels smiled. "Believe it or not, you're still considered to be in early labor. Even though it's the later stages of early labor. Once you hit seven centimeters, you'll be in active labor, which is more difficult to stop."

"So, we caught it early enough?" Georgia could hear the hope in her voice.

"It's hard to tell. We'll have to wait and see. It does get more difficult once a woman is in active labor."

"I see." Georgia felt hopeful. Maybe, just maybe, they could stop this.

"I'm going to perform an ultrasound shortly. I'm waiting for the machine to be brought up. In the meanwhile, I'm going to go ahead and give you a drug called Nifedipine to try to stop labor."

"I see," Georgia grunted the words. Another contraction was on its way.

"You're definitely under thirty-four weeks?" Doctor Michaels raised her brows in question. "It's very important. If you're not sure, then…"

"I'm sure," Georgia groaned, clutching at her belly. It was getting difficult to pay attention to what the doctor was saying.

Thankfully, she wrote in the file for a while, moving to the other side of the room to fetch something. Georgia stayed focused on her breathing. It didn't take long, and the contraction subsided.

"You're doing great," her doctor reassured her. "I'll go

ahead and give you Nefidipine now to try to stop the labor, and then steroids which are important for getting the baby's lungs more mature. Every minute will count. If we can hold things off until tomorrow, all the better."

"Shouldn't we wait until you perform the ultrasound?" Macy asked.

"It's more important that we hold off on delivering and that the baby's lungs mature. The sooner these drugs are administered the better. Like I said, pretty much every minute counts. If we find a problem on the ultrasound, we'll take it from there," Doctor Michaels said as she hung up a bag of IV fluids and had a needle in her gloved hands. Georgia hadn't seen her even put them on. "Are you righthanded or lefthanded?" she asked.

"Righthanded."

"Okay, we'll insert the IV on the left then." She tore open a small foil pack, and the scent of alcohol hit Georgia. She used the swab to clean the top of her hand. "You're going to feel a pinch," she warned before inserting the IV, taping it in place once she was done. Next, she handed Georgia a small cup. "Chew on the tablet."

Georgia did as she said. The medicine was bitter. Georgia must have made a face because Doctor Michaels handed her a glass of water. She gave a nod of thanks and took a deep drink.

"The next part is irritating but important. I need to inject you in your buttock. It will sting and the area might feel a little numb for a few minutes. It's the steroids to mature the baby's lungs."

Georgia leaned over on her side and felt a prick. Another contraction started up, so she didn't feel much after that since it hurt like hell. By the time she came back around, Doctor Michaels was standing next to a large piece of equipment. "We need to do an ultrasound, just to check what's going on in there. I'd like to measure the baby to get an exact indication of how far you are along. Also," she cleared her throat, "just to rule out any complications. It's routine," she added, "so, no need for concern."

"How exciting," Macy said. "Your first glimpse of the little one."

Shale was glowering heavily. He didn't look happy at all.

"Lift your gown to just below your breasts," Doctor Michaels requested. "That's it," she added, as Georgia did as she asked. She picked up a bottle and squeezed some clear gel onto Georgia's belly. It was surprisingly warm.

She placed the scanning wand thing onto her belly and turned to look at the screen. Then she frowned. "That's odd." Her eyes widened and then narrowed as she leaned forward towards the screen.

"What's wrong?" Georgia tried not to panic. She looked at the screen the doctor was staring at and it was black. Okay, not entirely black but almost. There were a couple of very dark gray areas. Otherwise, it was all dark.

Doctor Michaels moved the wand over her skin. She applied more of the gel on the other side and tried there. All with the same result. Splotchy and dark. Nothing to see.

"That's not right." The doctor fiddled with one or two of the dials and pushed a couple of buttons. "There's something wrong with the ultrasound machine. This has never happened before." She frowned harder. "I would love to try transvaginal but… we can't because your membranes have ruptured." She spoke more to herself, still moving the device over Georgia's belly in circular motions. She finally removed the wand altogether. "I can't perform the ultrasound right now. I'm going to have to call for another unit. Maybe the cardiac department has one to spare."

Her pains had started up again. Just when she began to relax from the last contraction another one would begin. Georgia grit her teeth. It didn't feel like those pills were working. Maybe it took time.

"Until then, we'll have to play it by ear. I'll send this machine through to maintenance. Although, I doubt they'll be able to do much onsite," her doctor went on, again talking more to herself.

"How bad is it that you can't… see inside me?" Georgia asked, gripping her belly.

"I prefer to get a look at what's going on in there. The good news is that you're pretty sure on the timelines. I'm hoping the Nifedipine works. Then we'll have time to perform an ultrasound later today. I really hope I can find another unit at such short notice. We like to check on things like placenta placement, the way the baby is lying. He… or she," the doctor pointed while looking at Shale and smiling, "could be lying breach or feet first. There are…"

Georgia struggled to keep up with the conversation after that. Doctor Michaels spoke for a few more seconds.

This contraction was worse than the ones before. It had been more severe and had lasted longer. Maybe that was just her imagination. Georgia slumped back against her pillow, breathing heavily. Whoever called this labor sure wasn't lying.

"Are you okay?" Shale looked concerned. "Is there anything I can do?"

She shook her head. Asking him to stop talking like a crazy person probably wouldn't help, so she refrained. *No point!*

Doctor Michaels had already left. "What did the doctor say? I missed the end bit of the conversation," Georgia asked, noticing that she was alone with Shale. "Where's Macy?"

"She went to the restroom." Shale gestured in that direction of the ward. "You don't have to worry. The babies are going to be just fine. Doctor Michaels said that a nurse is coming soon to bring you more medication." He made a face. "Anti-bio-tics." He said the word like it was foreign to him. "She also said there is a small possibility that you might need a C-section." He shrugged. "I'm not sure what that is."

Yeah, right! She decided to humor him. "It's when they operate to take the baby out because a—"

"It won't be necessary." He shook his head.

"You can't say that for sure." She looked at him like he had lost his marbles because, quite frankly… he had.

"I can!" Shale looked deadpan. He completely believed what he was saying. "Just like I know that no scanning equipment will work on you. Not with dragon whelps inside your—"

"Please, Shale… don't!" She put her fingers on her temples, pushing. "The equipment malfunctioned. That's all! It has nothing to do with anything else. I'm not pregnant with—"

"I'm not trying to scare you, Georgia. I know it's a lot

to take in, but—"

Just then the bathroom door opened. They both turned to look. Macy appeared. "How are you feeling?" her friend asked.

"I'm doing as well as can be expected," Georgia replied.

A nurse appeared in the doorway holding a tray with a couple of those plastic cups. She walked in and put the tray on the table.

"I'm Hillary," she announced, sounding as happy as sunshine and rainbows. "We need to monitor your contractions, as well as the baby's heartbeat. Doctor's orders. We'll use this." She held up a band with a device attached. Georgia had to lean forward while she attached the band around her belly. "Next, we plug it into this," she said, plugging a cord into a machine next to the bed.

The nurse – Hillary – pointed to a cup containing another pill, "I need you to take that in exactly six minutes."

Georgia smiled when she caught sight of the image on the machine's monitor.

"That's your baby's heartbeat. As you can see, nice and strong." The nurse beamed. She was a really sweet older lady who looked like she had a no-nonsense side to her as well. Georgia couldn't take her eyes off the moving blip on the screen. Her baby. He or she was doing well.

"The other medication on the tray is the antibiotic. You can take that now." She held the cup out to Georgia, and she took it, tipping the pills into her mouth and then drinking the water that was in the small cup.

"It's to keep infections at bay." The nurse smiled reassuringly.

A beep sounded on the machine and the needle spiked.

Georgia felt her belly harden as her uterus began to pull tight.

"This is what a contraction looks like," Hillary spoke to Shale and Macy. "I'm pretty sure you're going to need to chew on the Nifedipine tablet in a couple of minutes," she added, looking concerned.

"Does that mean the meds aren't working," Georgia managed to ground out, knowing the answer.

"Meds can sometimes take longer to kick in, sweetie, we'll know soon enough." She patted Georgia on the hand. "Take the Nifedipine once your contraction subsides. I'll be back in a half hour – call if you need me sooner. The button is over there." She gestured to somewhere behind Georgia, but the contraction was getting too strong to be able to respond. All she could do was breathe. That and pray.

CHAPTER 14

One hour later…

S weat beaded her brow. The contractions were coming one after the other with barely any time to catch her breath. There was no ultrasound machine available for the next hour, at least. They were doing this blind, which wasn't a problem, according to Doctor Michaels, who had looked tense when she'd informed them that the baby was coming. The drugs hadn't worked.

Macy put a straw to her lips. "Drink." Her friend's eyes were filled with concern.

Georgia's mouth felt dry and her lips were cracked, but she had barely taken one sip when the pains started up again. "Nooo!" she cried, exhaustion settling into her limbs. A feeling of hopelessness overtook her. This was wrong. The baby wasn't supposed to come just yet. The medication to stop the labor wasn't working. Twenty-six weeks. What did that even mean? How small would the little one be? *Oh, god!*

"Breathe." Shale took her hand and squeezed.

"No." She fought against the pain, against her own body. "I don't want this to happen. This can't happen!" The drugs were supposed to have stopped this. Why hadn't they? Her contractions were getting worse by the minute.

"Sorry to have to rain on your pity party," the doctor said, her eyes bearing into hers, "but this isn't over yet. You're nearly there. You should start to get the urge to push soon."

"I don't want to push! I can't have this baby." Tears spilled over.

"What you want or don't want doesn't count, I'm afraid. Nature has other ideas. Now breathe and try to relax. It won't help to fight."

Georgia sniffed, trying to hold back the tears. She nodded once, breathing with the contraction that wracked through her body.

"That's it!" Doctor Michaels said. "You are doing great." She moved between her splayed legs, checking her progress again. "You are nine centimeters. You will start to feel the need to bear down soon."

"I do feel more pressure down there." She bit down on her cracked lip, tasting the coppery tang of blood.

"Good. That means the little one is moving into the birthing canal. It won't be long, you're doing really well." The doctor gave her a smile. "The pediatrician is on his way. Shouldn't be more than a minute or two. He is really great at what he does. Being born so early is no longer the death sentence it once was. Ninety percent. Think about that."

Shale made a noise of irritation, which she ignored. He

kept insisting that the baby would be fine. Make that, *babies*. He hadn't let up.

The doctor went on. "You will have a difficult road ahead. The baby won't be able to go home with you but…"

Before Georgia could return the smile, pain rolled through her again, building with each panted breath. She clenched her teeth. In reality, a contraction lasted a minute, but it felt like forever. On the other hand, the two minutes between contractions seemed to go by in a heartbeat.

The pressure increased. Georgia felt the first tremors in her hands, and before long her whole body shook, like she had caught a chill or something. She was about to ask Doctor Michaels about it when the nurse arrived at her side. "It's normal to sometimes shiver like that. You're in what we call the transition phase of the labor. Your womb has opened, and the baby is slowly moving down, ready to be pushed out." She gave a reassuring smile. "You will continue to have contractions, they might get worse and closer together."

Worse!

How could this possibly get worse?

"Do you want more to drink?" Macy asked. It felt so good to know her friend was there with her.

Georgia shook her head. She felt exhausted. All she wanted to do was sleep. There would be no sleep for her for a good while. When the baby came – and it would be soon – she was going to be too worried to sleep. She blinked away more tears as they gathered. This was the time to be strong. Stronger than she had ever been in her life. She braced herself as another contraction took hold.

Georgia went from shivering to feeling too hot, and then back to shivering all over again. She kept having birthing pains. It was hard for Shale to watch and not to be able to do anything to help. They were so bad now that her back bowed and sweat dripped off of her. Shale wiped her forehead with a damp cloth and whispered words of encouragement. Truth was, he felt useless. He wanted to take her pain. To do something more for her, but what? There was nothing. All he could do was be there. It wasn't enough! Not nearly!

The healer went over to the foot of the bed once again, peering between Georgia's legs. She had done so twice already in the last half an hour.

Another healer was standing in the far side of the room. He had a whole lot of equipment set up and two nurses with him. They were waiting for the baby to be born and had explained that the infant would need to be put in a large box and taken away. Shale was not coping well with that thought. If they tried to take his sons, he wasn't sure what he would do. He might fight the male. It would be the wrong thing to do but his instincts were riding him hard.

"Your perineum is bulging." The doctor looked excited.

"Is that good or bad?" he blurted, unable to help himself. Georgia had slumped back onto the inclined section of the bed, panting heavily. When she turned her head, he noticed that her eyes were bloodshot. Her face was flushed and dripping with perspiration.

Her lips looked dry. "Shale…" Georgia's voice cracked.

He took her hand in his. "Do you need something?" He had a panicky edge to his voice.

She shook her head. "I'm scared. So scared. Right now, I'm hoping all those crazy things you said are true."

"They are true, Wisconsin." He squeezed her hand. "Everything I said is true. You'll see soon enough." Unfortunately, everyone in this room would see as well but there was nothing he could do about that at this point.

"A bulging perineum is good," the healer said. "The baby should start crowning soon."

She must have seen his look of confusion because she added. "The top of the baby's head will start to show soon."

Another pain hit. This time Georgia made these weird noises. "Oh, god!" she groaned. "I… I feel like pushing." She was out of breath, panting between every word.

The doctor was already at the foot of the bed. "You can push if you feel ready. Some women like sitting up, or on their haunches. You need to do what feels right. Make as much noise as you want. Do whatever it takes to help this along. I will guide you."

Georgia was making more of those strange noises. They were a deep kind of grunting. "I really need… I…" She was gritting her teeth.

"Do it!" the healer urged. "Push!"

Crunching her body as much as her swollen belly would allow, Georgia pushed. She drew in a deep breath and pushed again. She growled, snarled, panted and gripped his hand really tight – for a human – then she pushed some more.

When the contraction was finally over, she sagged back

against the pillow, panting hard.

Shale held her for a few moments.

"You're doing good, hun," Macy said in a hushed whisper. "I think you should wet your mouth. A nurse brought in some ice chips earlier." She held the bowl up to Georgia who sucked one. "Not too much," Macy added, "We don't want you getting ill. She warned of the possibility of that."

"Okay, Georgia. Let's get this baby out." The human rubbed her gloved hands together and leaned in between her legs.

"I'm so glad you're here," Georgia said between gritted teeth. She was looking at Macy when she said it. The two shared a moment. Shale felt like a useless asshole all over again. He didn't blame Georgia for not believing him. He sounded crazy to his own ears.

The whole pushing process started up again. She strained and strained, till her face turned red and sweat dripped from her forehead.

When it finally subsided, instead of falling back onto the bed, Georgia panted. "Help me up." She tried to get into a squatting position on the bed.

He shot a questioning look at the healer, who nodded. "It's fine. If she wants to sit up to have this baby, I'm good with that."

Shale lifted Georgia and carefully helped her into position on the bed. Georgia was unsteady, so he got in behind her bracketing her body with his arms to keep her in position. He put his back up against the headrest of the bed for support. "That's better," she sighed, almost sounding content. When the next birthing pain hit, she groaned loudly as she pushed. Her body was tense. Her heart raced.

"I can see the baby's head." The healer spoke calmly, but Shale could hear the excitement in her voice. "Listen to me carefully, I need you to stop pushing now."

"But I have to push," Georgia argued.

"I don't want you to tear," the doctor said. "We need to take it slow. You're stretching too quickly."

Georgia shook her head, continuing to push with all her might. "Have to," she ground the words out between clenched teeth.

"You are going to tear," the healer warned. "Stop! Breathe instead."

"O-okay," Georgia grit out, sounding unsure. "I'll try," she whimpered.

"I know it's tough, but you can do it," the healer continued. "That's it. You're doing great."

"I can't!" Georgia yelled. "Need to… must… can't," she groaned.

"No, you need to give your perineum time to stretch or there's a good chance you'll tear badly. Trust me, you don't want that. The infant is bigger than I expected." She said the last to herself, sounding shocked.

He felt her tremble in his arms. Georgia whimpered again. She truly sounded like she was in agony. Which she most probably was. Shale's sense of uselessness mounted, until he remembered something stupid from his Google searches the night before. *It might help.* "Blow out the candle," he blurted.

"What?" both Georgia and Macy said in unison.

"Pretend there is a candle a few inches from your mouth. Blow it out. Do it now."

Thankfully, she didn't question him. Georgia was probably too desperate at that stage. He heard her blow.

"Okay," he said, holding onto her arms, supporting her as much as he could. "It's one of those candles that reignites itself. Blow it out again."

She sucked in a breath and blew. They went through this process two more times.

"Okay." The doctor was doing something between Georgia's legs. He couldn't see. "You can push again."

Georgia did as she said, bearing down hard. She grunted low and deep.

"That's it," Shale said, watching as the healer's eyes lit with excitement.

Georgia held onto his forearms, she made a growl of frustration as the contraction subsided.

"Your baby is right there. One or two more good pushes and he will be born."

Georgia was leaning back against him, she nodded. "Okay." She was panting heavily.

"Standing by," the male healer announced, moving in closer. "My team and I are ready."

"Great! This is Doctor Hickstead." The healer looked back their way. "Just so you know," she addressed Georgia, "it is normal for an infant to move down and pull back up. It's fine, just as long as they keep moving down in the long run. I think your perineum is stretched sufficiently, but if I tell you to stop again, you need to listen, okay?"

"I understand." Georgia was slumped in his arms. She sounded exhausted. Macy was there giving her more liquids.

"Good move," the healer said, looking at him. "I'm going to remember the candle thing. Haven't heard that one before."

Georgia's breathing hitched and her body began to tense in preparation for the next contraction.

"Are you ready to meet your baby?" The healer smiled.

Georgia nodded, "It's too late now to say no," she forced out before a low growl began to build in her throat.

"Good." The healer looked down. "Push now, Georgia, push!"

Shale held onto her, wishing so hard that he could do something more to help her through this.

Georgia's loud groan turned into a triumphant shout.

The healer looked really busy. "Your baby's head is out. I'm just cleaning the nasal passage and checking to ensure that the mouth is clear. There is no umbilical cord around the neck. The infant is small but looks... good." She sounded surprised. The other healer moved in closer, his whole stance showing readiness.

Without thinking about it, Shale nuzzled into the back of her hair, damp with sweat. He inhaled her scent. "I'm so proud of you." His first son was almost there. Pride burst from his chest.

Georgia trembled in his arms. "Is he okay?" she whispered. "Is he... is he...?"

"He looks good. On the next contraction, we'll free his shoulders," the healer responded.

Georgia sighed.

"Here we go!" the doctor shouted.

Georgia stiffened. All it took was one big push and their whelp was in the healer's arms. The baby squirmed and kicked while the healer cut the cord. He couldn't see much of what was happening from his angle behind Georgia. The nurse helped.

"Oh, my goodness," the human said. "You were right," she glanced up at Shale, "it's a boy." The little one squirmed some more. He let out a wail. It was loud and strong and filled Shale with joy like he had never felt before.

Georgia laughed. It had a hysterical edge. "He's okay then?" Tears coursed down her cheeks. "He's breathing, isn't he?"

"Yes, he is," the healer said, still busy with his whelp.

Shale kept supporting Georgia as much as he could. When she tried to get up, he held her in place. It wouldn't be long before her pains began again. Before the urge to push started up again. She might not know it, but that moment would be on her soon.

The male healer took his whelp from Doctor Michaels and Shale had to stop himself from snarling. Males were not permitted in the birthing chamber back at the lair. Recently, fathers had been present for the birth of their whelps. It seemed that human females preferred it that way. Outside males, however… forget about it. Every possessive instinct flared up in him, his lip curled away from his teeth in a silent snarl and his scales rubbed beneath his skin.

"Are you okay, Shale?" Macy asked.

He nodded once, keeping his eyes on the male healer who held his son. The male rushed over to the table on the far said of the room, placing his son on a mat. The healer got to work right away. It looked like he was suctioning the baby's nose and mouth with some or other device. There was a slurping noise. Shale was torn. He wanted to go to his whelp, but he also needed to stay with Georgia. A nurse stood close by, handing the healer tools. The doctor made the odd comment, using terms Shale had never heard before. He could hear his son breathing. Could hear the rhythm of their whelp's heart.

CHAPTER 15

Her heart practically beat out of her chest. Her soul felt like it might burst. Georgia strained to see what was happening and caught a glimpse of her tiny baby. Just a glimpse. She whimpered, putting a hand to her chest. Right then she felt every emotion there was to feel. They all ran through her. Each one fighting for center stage. She felt absolute elation. Then fear... more fear than she imagined possible. She also felt frustration and anger. *Why had this happened?* Her baby was going to have to fight for his life. He was going to have to fight for every breath. She caught another fleeting glimpse just as the pediatrician put her son on a table. He was shouting to his staff for equipment. The baby wasn't quite as small as she expected he would be. She'd seen pictures of premature babies and they always looked odd. Very big heads and paper-thin, wrinkly skin. For the few seconds she had seen him, her son appeared to be normal. His skin had been pink. Not blue. It didn't mean anything. He was premature. It was what it was.

"Please," Georgia moaned the word, "is my baby okay?"

"He's fine," Shale murmured. "I swear he is."

Then there was a gasping noise and a tiny squeak. Her son was alive. He was very much alive. She'd seen him kicking and squirming. He was fighting. She could hear it and sense it. Her son was a fighter. Then her heart sank.

Her son.

Her baby.

Hers.

She needed to stop thinking of him in those terms. Georgia needed to contact the Joyces. She needed to let them know what had happened. They deserved to know.

"He's beautiful," Macy gushed. There were tears running down her friend's cheeks. "I can't believe how strong you are," she added, looking at Georgia. "I'm sure your little boy is going to be just fine."

"He's not mine." She tried to sound resolute and was both happy and unhappy to say that she succeeded.

"He *is* yours." Shale's arms tightened around her, making her realize that she was still in his arms, on the bed. "He's yours, Georgia. You're his mother."

Tears began to fall all over again. "Please make sure he's okay?" she asked Macy, feeling a lump in her own throat. Georgia needed to hold it together. She wiped her eyes and sniffed hard.

Macy walked to where they were still working on their son. One of the nurses stopped her. "Please stand to the side. Let the doctor do his job."

"Please listen," another nurse added, using a voice of

authority.

"Please let me see him," Georgia pleaded, trying to see what they were doing. "At least let me know how he's doing."

There was so much activity. She thought she heard another squeak. "Let my female see our son," Shale growled. His fists were clenched and his jaw was tight.

"Let me get up," she whispered.

Shale shook his head. "You aren't done yet."

"The placenta will come when it's ready," the doctor commented, overhearing them. "It might have a few minutes yet. You shouldn't feel much. Maybe a light contraction at the most. You're nearly done." She went to fetch something from a set of drawers.

He shook his head. "I'm not talking about your... placenta," he said under his breath. "You are going to birth another whelp." He spoke so softly that she could hardly hear him.

Whelp!

What?

More mumbo jumbo. It was so frustrating. Just when Shale seemed completely normal, just when she started to feel comfortable with him, he would say something along these lines. Dragons, lairs and whelps. She rubbed her eyes, feeling exhausted.

Georgia tried to get up again, she needed to go to her son. Her baby needed her, but Shale held onto her.

Frustration ate at her. "How is he?" she tried again, louder this time. Her throat hurt.

Macy tried to give her some more ice chips, but she shook her head. She suddenly felt a touch of nausea. That, and very cold. The placenta must be coming soon. It almost felt like she was about to have another contraction. "How is my baby?" she asked again, louder this time.

The doctor ignored her. He kept on working for another half a minute. It could have been less than that because each second felt like a lifetime. Then he held up her son. Finally.

Georgia gasped at how beautiful he was. Tiny, but not as small as she thought. She had been right about that. He was perfect in every other aspect. One little foot gave a tiny kick and she sobbed, tears coursing down her cheeks. "He looks like he's breathing fine."

"He's two point five one pounds," the doctor said. "You were most likely further along than you realized." He smiled. "Your son is breathing well. I'm baffled, actually. How long did you say the patient was on steroids for, Doctor Michaels?"

"A couple of hours." Doctor Michaels sounded shocked as well.

"Well, that might be it. Certainly worked at maturing his lungs. He has some kind of... I don't know... birthmark on his chest." She could see that both pediatricians were frowning heavily. "It's the strangest thing. It looks..."

Then it hit and hard, almost knocking the air from her lungs. A contraction. She would have doubled over if Shale hadn't held onto her. As it was, she hunched forward, making a harsh groaning noise that hurt her throat. She couldn't stop it from happening. *What the hell?*

Georgia didn't know much about childbirth. What she did know was that contractions after the baby was born were supposed to slow down to a minimum. Some women reported not even feeling them anymore when pushing out the placenta. It wasn't supposed to feel like this. Or was it? Georgia wanted to ask Doctor Michaels, but she couldn't talk. She focused on her breathing instead.

Doctor Michaels looked concerned. "Are you alright, Georgia?"

Georgia managed to shake her head. What was that the pediatrician had said about a strange birthmark? Where had he said it was? If only it didn't hurt so much. She'd be able to think. Something rattled around in her brain, but she couldn't put two and two together. She groaned as the pain intensified. Then she felt—

"Oh, good lord! Oh, heck…" she groaned.

"You shouldn't be… contractions…" She caught splintered parts of what Doctor Michaels was saying to her. Her doctor was examining her. Checking her heart-rate.

She finally looked between her legs and jumped up like a jack-in-the-box, eyes wide. Georgia's contraction subsided. Her pain slowly easing off. "What is it?' she panted the words.

"Your perineum is bulging." Doctor Michaels swallowed. "I think…"

Georgia turned back to look at Shale. "It's true! I'm having twins." Her heart was beating so wildly it felt like it might just bruise her ribcage.

He nodded once. "Yep. That's what I've been trying to tell you."

"All of it's true?" She sounded skeptical. Heck, she still *felt* skeptical. It would mean that he was a dragon shifter. A freaking dragon. How was that possible?

He nodded again, giving her a half-smile. "Every last thing I told you is true. All of it."

"No way!" Macy yelled, sounding shocked.

That meant that he was a prince. Her babies… not baby, *babies*… Her eyes felt wide. Her blood felt like it had drained from her body. Maybe that's why her heart was beating overtime. "Shit," she mumbled. Georgia could feel her belly begin to tighten. "Help me back up."

Shale did as she asked, lifting and then maneuvering her into position easily.

"You're having twins, alright," Doctor Michaels piped up. "The second one will crown and may even be born on your next contraction."

She nodded.

"With twin births, normally everything goes quicker the second time around. The first baby paves the way for the second."

Georgia was struggling to hear what Doctor Michaels was saying. "I need to push," she ground out.

"Do it!" her doctor said, looking from between her legs to her face and back again.

Shale held her tightly. "You can do this," he urged.

Georgia pushed with all her might, feeling immense pressure between her legs. It hurt, but it also felt good to push. Like finally being able to scratch an itch.

The pressure built and built and then in one rush was gone as her baby was born.

"Good job!" Doctor Michaels was smiling. "Another son. He also looks very healthy." The nurse was there, handing Doctor Michaels clamps and scissors.

"I paged Doctor Greene," the pediatrician announced.

Her son made a wailing noise. She could hear him suck in a deep breath. Georgia sagged against Shale. Her boys were part dragon shifter. They weren't human. That meant that they *were* full-term like Shale had said. They were going to be just fine. She couldn't stop smiling. "He has red hair," she muttered.

"They both do," Shale chuckled, sounding excited. "Gorgeous like their mom." She could hear he was still smiling. "You did it," he said, kissing her temple. "You're amazing." His voice sounded choked.

"Oh, my gosh!" Macy clapped her hands softly. "You have two babies. Two!" She laughed. "I can't believe it. Can you believe it? Oh my god, but I'm in awe over here."

She felt Shale tense when their second born was handed over to the pediatrician who had just arrived. He was out of breath and his coat buttons had been done up wrong. "It'll be okay," she tried to soothe him. *Shale. A dragon shifter. Shit!* This was surreal. It was completely mind-blowing.

"You can't take them," Shale pretty much growled the words. His chest actually vibrated against her back.

Their firstborn was nestled in the incubator. The pediatrician was still busy with baby number two. "They won't do anything to harm them," she tried again. "I just realized I don't have names. I don't even have a name for one of them, let alone two. I don't have anything for them. No diapers. No—"

"Don't worry," Shale said as he stood up. He lifted her back and into a better position. "Everything will be taken care of. Everything will be fine." He pushed some hair behind her ear. "We'll come up with their names together."

Georgia had so many questions. She burned to ask them all, but couldn't. Her belly was contracting lightly. It was almost indiscernible after the last couple of contractions. It most likely indicated that the placenta was coming. She couldn't get back up, even though she wanted to go and check on her babies.

Both of her sons were put into the incubator. "I must say, we are shocked at how well these two are doing," Doctor Hickstead said. "They are identical twins. They even have that same birthmark. It's... bizarre. I've never seen anything like it. There are laser treatments available, so I wouldn't worry. Otherwise, they seem to be extremely healthy."

"You most certainly were further along with this pregnancy," the other pediatrician commented. "There is no alternate explanation," he stated, shaking his head. Georgia couldn't remember his name. "That, plus the steroids taking effect after such a short period of time, means that your boys are in good health and breathing well on their own. For now, the incubator is oxygenated, and the temperature is regulated."

"We are going to take them—" Doctor Hickstead began.

"No!" Shale snarled.

The first doctor paled and the second even took a step back, clutching his chest.

"B-but... um—" Doctor Hickstead stammered.

"But nothing!" Shale's voice was booming. His hands were fisted at his sides. He looked ready to tear the two of them limb from limb. He was quite capable of doing it too. Being that he was a shifter. Georgia still couldn't believe it. There was no other logical explanation. He had known things he couldn't possibly know. Twins, chest markings, boys. It had to be.

"You n-need to let us d-do our jobs," Doc Two

stammered, taking another step back and lifting a hand as if to ward Shale off.

"We will need to run further tests," Doctor Hickstead spoke carefully. "Just to be on the safe side. It is important that we check for oxygen saturation, that the infants have the suck reflex."

"Exactly!" Doc Two stated, with more confidence now that his colleague had stepped forward. "We need to monitor them over a period to make sure they remain stable. Then, we can make a call as to whether or not they will be able..."

"They should be with their mother." Shale clenched his jaw.

Her heart hurt at the prospect of them taking her babies. It physically hurt, but this was a necessary step. "Um... Shale," Georgia reached up and took his hand, "let the doctors do their job. Why don't you go with them? Keep an eye on things."

Doctor Hickstead shook his head, pulling in a breath. "That won't be neces—"

"I would have to insist," Shale growled. "Otherwise, my children are not going anywhere." He folded his arms, towering over the two doctors.

"Okay then." Doctor Hickstead nodded.

"Charles, what are you...?" Doc Two began.

"We don't seem to have much of a choice," Doctor Hickstead said, eyes wide and still trained on Shale.

"Alright." Doc Two shook his head in disgust. "You will need to stay out of the way."

"I'll... we'll be back as soon as we can." Shale squeezed her hand and then leaned down and kissed her on the forehead. It was platonic. It was friendly and sweet, but butterflies still took wing in her stomach. This, despite another mild contraction and an irritating need to push. It wasn't like before. Nothing major, just an irritation.

"Yes, you go. I'll be fine. Just…" Shale turned back. "Don't hurt anyone. They're only trying to help our boys."

Our boys.

What was she saying? Georgia was assuming that they were going to be one happy family. Not together as a couple, but parents to this baby. That might not happen.

The whole business of pushing out the placenta lasted less than ten seconds. "I'm happy to announce that you didn't tear," Doctor Michaels said. "The placenta looks complete. We'll be able to discharge you in a day or two. It doesn't seem like your sons will need to be here all that long either, but you'll have to wait to hear from Doctor Hickstead and Doctor Greene on that note."

"Thank you." Georgia smiled.

"I'm so glad things turned out so well," Doctor Michaels said as she pulled off the rubber gloves. "Someone will be in to wheel you to your private room shortly."

"Private?" Her eyes widened. Private rooms were costly.

"Yes." Her doctor nodded. "Your partner insisted on it."

"Private rooms cost lots of money!" She couldn't fathom the idea.

"He's already paid for everything in full." Doctor Michaels winked at her.

Holy crap, this was really happening?

"I'll come through and check on you when I make my rounds later. Otherwise, get some rest. Your life is about to become really busy." She choked out a laugh. "I can't believe you didn't know you were carrying twins. It's never happened to me in my whole career."

"I can't believe it either."

"Push the call bell if you need anything. The nurses will check up on you regularly. Oh, and it's the most bizarre thing. Maintenance got back to me and the ultrasound machine seems to be working just fine again." She shook her head. "We'll have to keep an eye on it. I can't believe this happened." She grinned. "I'm so glad you guys are all doing so well."

Georgia nodded. "Me too, thanks." More proof that everything Shale had said was the truth. That he was completely sane.

They watched as Doctor Michaels left. Macy clapped her hand over her mouth and laughed hysterically. "I can't believe what just happened," she finally said. "It's all true, isn't it?" Her eyes were wide.

Georgia nodded. "I think so."

"I mean, you had twins with chest markings. They're both boys who are, it would seem, absolutely fine." She wiped a hand over her face. "Shale is a shifter." She said the last under her breath. "Not just that, he's a prince."

"I still struggle to believe it. I just…"

"And he told you he wants the two of you to raise these children?" Macy asked, sitting on the edge of her bed.

Georgia nodded. "I don't want to get my hopes up just yet. I have no idea what all of this means." She shrugged. "I just can't comprehend. I was just starting to come to terms with the Joyces adopting my child. Now I have two, and the father is here and wanting to… be their father."

"And he's not human." Macy mouthed '*OMG.*'

"It's all surreal." She pushed out a heavy breath.

"Do you think he wants the two of you to be, not just parents to the boys, but an item?" Macy raised her brows.

"I doubt it very much." She shook her head hard. "It was a one-night thing. I can't see it playing out like that. Like I said, we have a lot to talk through."

"Would you be interested… in Shale in that way?" Macy asked, her voice animated. "I mean, if he was interested in you in that way? You guys could be a family."

"Slow it down, there. He's a good-looking guy and I'm attracted to him, but I doubt there's any more there… between us. I don't think he's the settling down type."

"Up until a few days ago, you didn't think he was father material either, and yet here he is growling at the doctors and being very much a father. He wouldn't take his eyes off those little boys. He was sweet with you too, during the labor. So sweet! I would love a guy like that."

Georgia felt her eyes well. "He *was* pretty sweet, and my babies are beautiful, aren't they?"

"So beautiful," Macy gushed. "They look just like you." Her friend smiled broadly.

They both laughed. "Gingers," Georgia said, between her laughter and tears. "I wish I could hold them." Her laughter turned into a sob.

"Oh, hun." Macy put her arms around her. "I'm willing to bet that Shale will have them in your arms in no time."

They let each other go. "You're right." Georgia nodded. "I have a big favor to ask."

"Your mom." Macy smiled. "I'm headed there as soon as I leave here, which," she looked at her watch, "needs to be right now."

"You're a lifesaver."

"I know." She smiled broadly. "You will owe me, big time."

"Most definitely."

"I'll come and visit after work tomorrow."

Georgia nodded. "That would be lovely."

"I can't wait to hold those little bundles of joy myself. Get Shale to take lots of pics of all of you guys."

Georgia narrowed her eyes. "You should stop with all of that. It's not going to be like that between us."

"I saw that kiss he planted on your forehead earlier." She grinned. It was all out wicked.

"Exactly. Nowhere near the lips. Go already." She shooed Macy.

Her friend chuckled as she headed to the door.

"Don't forget, if my mom's in one of her moods you will need to—"

"I know…" Macy turned back smiling. "I'll clean the room until she calms down."

"And if she's lucid…" The idea worried her more because her mom would worry where she was.

"I'll handle it," Macy said.

"I'm not sure if you should tell her what's going on."

"Of course I will tell her. She'll want to know," Macy insisted.

"I don't know if that's wise. She'll get upset. She'll cry. You know how she becomes when she realizes how much she's missed. Even worse, how much she's deteriorated."

"Your mom is a grandmother. She will want to know. Let me be the judge of her mood. Chances are good I'll clean for half an hour and then head home. Teddy will be dying to go for a walk. Hopefully he hasn't chewed up my sofa." Macy rolled her eyes.

"You wanted a puppy." Georgia smiled back.

"I love him to bits," her friend said, smiling. "I'll see you tomorrow. I can't wait to hear all about it and to meet those gorgeous boys of yours."

"I can't wait either." Her voice hitched. They hugged and Macy left.

CHAPTER 16

Three hours later…

Shale handed their eldest son to his mother. Georgia was crying openly. A smile on her lips. Her eyes were focused on the bundle in her arms. "He's so little and so perfect." She looked his way, smiling. "I can't believe this. I just can't!" She shook her head, her eyes glistening.

"He is all of those things," Shale agreed, looking on. Georgia put their boy down in her lap, gazing down at him.

The little one yawned. "He's so adorable." Georgia touched her finger against his hand, and he gripped it. She chuckled. "So clever. He has your eyes."

"They both do." Shale felt such pride. He never believed he would ever feel this way. Love beyond compare. Their youngest son was sleeping soundly in a crib next to the bed.

"Oh, does he?" Her eyes were wide as she looked over at their sleeping whelp.

"Yep. They have your hair and my eyes."

She bit down on her lip. "You're not upset, are you?"

He blinked. "About what?"

"That they have my hair. Ginger isn't for everyone."

"Are you kidding, Wisconsin? I love your fiery red hair. I've told you that before. You have given me two perfect sons. I couldn't be happier."

Her face turned a deep pink color which highlighted her green eyes.

The baby squirmed, making a choking, crying sound. His little face began to turn red.

Her face morphed into one of shock. That and a touch of panic. "What's wrong?" Georgia asked, eyes wide. "I didn't read any books about taking care of babies. I'm clueless! I had planned on giving my baby up for adoption. I stayed away from that part of the thinking process. It was too painful."

Shale felt everything in him tighten. He clenched his jaw. "That's not happening. You don't—"

"We have a lot to talk about but..." A tear leaked from her eye. "I love my babies... so much. I never wanted to give them up. It wasn't—"

"I know, and things have changed. Your position has changed."

"You don't know everything." She shook her head, her wild tangle of curls tumbling down her back. "Things have changed, and yet, some things haven't. I'm so afraid to allow myself to hope. I feel so much for both my babies already. We don't know each other. You don't know..." The baby fussed some more, his little legs kicking quicker and harder. Georgia picked him up, holding him against her. Her eyes were filled with worry. She patted his back, but he continued to squirm. His little whimpers and cries growing louder. "Am I holding him wrong?"

"I think he's hungry."

"Hungry?" Georgia's eyes were so wide it was almost comical.

"Yes. It happens," Shale said. "You should…" He looked pointedly at her breasts.

"Oh… ohhhh!" The baby was nuzzling into her chest and then wailing. "Um… I have no idea how to do this. I need a book or a nurse, or…" She was looking around her, trying to find the call button.

"You're his mother. You know what to do, just as he does. It's instinctual."

Georgia was breathing fast. Her heart-rate was elevated as well. In short, she was terrified.

"I'll help you," he added, having to raise his voice above the increasingly louder cries of their baby.

"Because you're an expert in breastfeeding."

Shale shrugged. He'd seen it done enough times over the last few years. He had witnessed a sister and the mates of two brothers raise babies.

"I guess you know a lot about breasts since you are somewhat of a player." She raised her brows. "So maybe you can help me." She laughed at her own joke, quickly turning serious when the baby choked out another cry.

"Actually, I have a couple of nephews and nieces running around. My family is close."

She swallowed thickly. "O-okay. I'll try it." Georgia put her hand behind her gown, trying to untie the back.

"Here, I'll do that." He helped her with it.

She was a natural. Georgia pulled down the gown over one shoulder and put their whelp to her breast. The little one was both greedy and a complete natural too. Within seconds, he was drinking noisily. "I think he might take after his father." Shale couldn't help but grin as he watched his tiny son nurse.

"What? He's a breast man?" She smiled, also looking down as well.

"I was thinking more along the lines of having a healthy appetite but… yeah," he chuckled, "that too." Shale was trying hard not to notice her plump breasts. It would be so damned wrong in this situation. "We do need to talk. Maybe now would be a good time."

"Okay." She nodded, looking more worried than when she didn't know what to do with the baby.

"I need you to come back with me to my lair. Back to dragon lands. I promise it's all quite civilized."

"Um… wow! That was unexpected." She shook her head.

"I'm sorry. I probably should have led up to that part, but I've never been all that good with small talk. The babies aren't human. They don't belong here." He looked around them. "I want all three of you to come back with me. I will be able—"

"I can't." Just like that. No thinking about it. No talking it through. He had expected push back but not a definite 'no' right off the bat.

"I don't expect anything from you in the way of a relationship. Don't be concerned about that." He put up a hand. "I understand that playing happy family and trying to be a couple isn't going to work. You'd have your own space and…"

Shale swore that for a second, she looked disappointed, and whether it was because she wanted to come back with him, or because she had hoped for more with him, he wasn't sure. The look was gone almost as soon as it arrived.

"It's not that." She pushed out a breath. "I told you I have responsibilities... here in Dalton Springs, and I meant it. I can't up and leave. It's just not a possibility."

"What responsibilities?" He was sure he could take care of them. Whatever they were. However big she thought they were. "I know you said you work two jobs, but you don't need to anymore."

"I can't just quit."

"You can. If it will make you feel better, I'll have my lawyers draw up a contract." He paused, trying to think of the right wording. "I'll pay you... child support? Is that the right terminology? I want you to be there for them. You are their mother. I am their father. It is my responsibility. It would not be a handout or anything like that. I hope you don't think that."

"No, I don't. I want to be there for them, and child support would be amazing. You have no idea how amazing, but..." Her shoulders slumped, and tears leaked out from the corners of her eyes. Georgia sniffed, wiping at her face with one hand while the other cradled their still nursing son. "I can't possibly up and leave. I have to take care of my mother."

"Your mother?" He frowned. "Is she elderly? Does she live with you? She could come with us."

Georgia smiled. Her lashes were still wet. Her eyes were extra shiny with unshed tears. "That's so sweet." She shook her head. "I can't believe how sweet you have been."

"What? For a 'player'?"

"Something like that." Her smile widened. "I didn't expect it. That's all." Then another tear leaked over. "My mom is sick. I need to keep working to pay her medical expenses. If I'm working, I can't be a mom to these babies. I've explored it from all angles and it's just not going to be possible to—"

"I told you I'm going to cover your expenses. All of them."

"For the babies, which is great! I would never expect you—"

"Not just the babies, Georgia. I'll cover whatever expenses you have." He tried to keep his voice calm, even though he was beginning to feel desperate.

"Hold on." She raised a hand. "You don't know what you're saying." She shook her head. "My mother has Alzheimer's." She must have seen the look on his face because she went on to explain. "It's a neurodegenerative disease that affects… essentially, the brain." She shrugged. "It causes dementia, mood swings, memory loss, disorientation and behavioral issues. And it slowly develops until basic bodily functions are lost. It is eventually fatal." She wiped at her eyes again. "My mom is in a home. She was diagnosed three years back and has slowly deteriorated. She's been in a home for the last… almost a year now. She mostly doesn't even know who I am anymore. We have the occasional good day."

"I'm so sorry." What else did he say to all that? He wanted to say more but had no words.

"She needs constant round-the-clock care by professionals. Dealing with someone like my mom is not easy. She struggles to express herself and is prone to violence at times. She needs to be dressed and fed and has to be monitored constantly. She is a danger to herself and others. She can't leave the home she's in, and I can't leave her... I just can't. I'm all she has." Her voice was a touch shrill and more tears coursed down her cheeks.

Fuck! His chest felt tight. No wonder she had been so wound up six months ago. No wonder she was wound up now. No wonder she had felt like giving the babies up for adoption was her only option.

The baby stopped nursing, Georgia put him over her shoulder and began patting his back softly. Doing exactly the right thing without even thinking about it. Shale helped her fix her gown. His mind running a mile a minute. "The thing is, the babies can't stay in Dalton Springs. They can't stay amongst humans." He sat back down. "There is a good reason why the dragons have chosen to keep our existence a secret. For years, we've been hunted by a band of humans. The stories you hear about knights hunting and killing dragons... they're not just stories. We were hunted to near extinction. Our sons are not safe here. The hunters are far more sophisticated nowadays. They have money, and lots of it. They also have spies everywhere." He looked into her large, green eyes. "I know this all sounds unbelievable."

"I *do* believe you. It was tough before, but not now," she shook her head, "not after they were born. It's surreal, but I do believe you."

"Good! Thank you. Thing is, the hunters know what to look for. Chest markings are a dead giveaway. Our boys will be safe on dragon lands, amongst their own. I want you to come with us."

"So, you're asking me to choose all over again." She shook her head. "To choose between my mom and my children." Her shoulders shook and she put a hand over her face which had crumpled. Then she sniffed. "I'm sorry. I thought it was a no-brainer but now that they are here…" She cradled their son in her arms, looking down at him with such love and affection. Such sorrow.

Shale cleared his throat. "I would never expect you to choose. We do need to leave within the next hour though. I have already secured a helicopter. Are you well enough to travel? I would imagine that you would be. Your healing capabilities will be higher than normal after carrying dragon whelps inside you."

"Are they? Higher than normal that is?" He could see that her mind was racing. She pushed out a breath. "Oh, god! You're right! My healing capabilities *are* better." She thought back to the papercut, and if she was honest with herself there had been other incidences. "I can travel… yes but…"

He could see her shutting down. "Please, Georgia, come with us. I'm worried about you too. You might become a target if they suspect you birthed dragon whelps. They'd use you to get to me. These people are ruthless. Once we are safe, I'll figure something out. I'm sure we can find a solution that will work for your mother."

"For how long? I visit my mom every day. She needs me. I can't just abandon her. I can't abandon them either." She looked back down at the babies.

"It wouldn't be for long. I promise you that." He sounded desperate but he didn't care.

Their second-born gave a yell. His little feet kicked. His eyes were still closed but he was clearly waking up. "I think someone else needs to be fed as well," Shale said. "They need you Georgia, please. I swear we'll find a solution that works for us all. We'll share my apartment, but you'll have your own room. If it takes more than a couple of days to sort things out, I'll take you to see your mom. It's safer this way."

She handed him their sleeping baby. Shale put the little one down, picking up the other, now squirming, yelling bundle. He untied her gown. "You should put him on your other breast. I heard one of my brother's mates talking and that's how it supposedly works. You should switch sides. It's easier if you feed them both at once. I'll buy us a couple of parenting guides."

"You seem to know what you're doing," she remarked, putting their baby to her breast. He quickly nuzzled in and began drinking.

"So do you." He soothed the fuzzy, red hair on his tiny head, using two fingers. "What do you say, Iowa? Are you willing to try it?"

"You promise to take me to see my mom if it takes too long?" She was frowning heavily. "I'm so worried she's lucid and realizes I haven't been there. She'll worry. It's what mothers do, and she's still... my mom." He could see that she was working hard to hold it together. "I'm *their* mom, though. They need me too." Her lip quivered.

"I promise I'll take you to see her. Hopefully, I'll have a solution quickly." He needed to run a couple of ideas past his brother. Blaze might need to approve some things as well.

"Also," she chewed on her bottom lip, "I supplement my mother's care. Half of what I earn goes towards her treatment." She looked up for a moment. "I could keep working from wherever it is that we're going," she said, more to herself. "I can still design covers. Please tell me you have internet connection back at your lair. I would be happy to contribute—"

"I will take care of all your expenses and all of your needs. That includes your mother's care. You do not have to worry. You do not have to work."

"I can't just give everything up."

"I'll draw up that contract. You will not have to worry financially."

"That's not fair. My mom is my—"

"I want the mother of my children safe. I want all of your focus on our whelps. No stress or worries. I have money, Georgia. You no longer have to work." *How to convey this?*

He saw the column of her throat work. "I don't know how I feel about that."

"We'll figure it out. Once the three of you are safe, we'll talk about it." She was used to fending for herself. Not having anyone in her corner. That was about to change.

She nodded once. "Okay." She didn't look too convinced though. "Can we go back to my place to pack?"

"No, I'm sorry but we need to head out. I have called ahead and have already made arrangements. There will be clothing and items for the babies. We can go past your house in a couple of days when we visit with your mother."

She nodded.

Shale pushed out a sigh of relief. For a second there he was sure she was going to argue with him some more.

"I need to call the Joyces and let them know." Georgia's face dropped. "I'm so happy this is working out for us, but I feel terrible for them. Just awful. They're such a nice couple."

"You hadn't made any promises yet?" Trust Georgia to put everyone before her own needs.

She shook her head. "Not yet, but I know they had their hopes up."

"I'm sure they'll find a baby to adopt."

"I really hope so."

"It will all work out." He touched the side of her arm. "You'll see." He wasn't talking about the Joyces. He was talking about them. Shale only hoped that he was right. They didn't know each other very well at all. Was there still something between them? A spark that could become more? Or had their relationship run its course? Only time would tell.

CHAPTER 17

Georgia needed to pick her jaw up off the floor, but she couldn't. It just wasn't possible. "Oh, my god! Oh, my—" She bit down to keep from saying every known swear word under the sun. "That's a dragon. An honest to god—Oh!" she half-yelled. "There's another one." She laughed. The beasts were huge and yet graceful. Their great wings flapping. Their scales glinted in the sunlight.

Shale chuckled, it sounded crackly through the earphones. "There are a lot more of us."

"Wow! Dragon shifters are bigger than I expected… I mean, in your dragon form. Very pretty."

"Pretty?" Shale choked out a laugh. "Don't let any of the males hear you calling them pretty and don't you dare call me pretty in my dragon form."

"You wish!" she muttered smiling. "Oh, god!" She covered her mouth with her hand. Her jaw had dropped all over again, and she couldn't seem to pick it up this time.

"It's something, isn't it?" She could hear the affection in Shale's voice, which, again, crackled through her earphones.

"That's your lair?" Her words were laced with wonder.

"Yep," Shale said.

"When you said lair, I imagined it would be a hole in the ground or something. Okay," she quickly added, "maybe not quite a hole in the ground, but I did not expect this. Even the views are breathtaking." The lair was cut into the side of a cliff. It was all glass and stone and was breathtaking, with views over the coastline and the ocean.

"You should see the Water dragons' lair," Storm piped up. He was flying the helicopter they were currently in.

Shale chuckled. "Bullshit. A lair is a lair."

Storm chuckled as well. He was a Water dragon prince. Just like Shale was an Earth dragon prince. There were also Fire dragons and… Air dragons. Her mind was boggled.

"Hold on," Storm said. "I'm taking her down." Each of them held one of the babies. Shale had decided it would be better if they took a helicopter into dragon lands instead of shifting and flying in.

The chopper slowly descended onto a large balcony area that jutted off the lair. It took a minute or two for the chopper to power down. Thankfully, the babies were still sleeping soundly. They had put cotton wool in their ears. She'd had to feed their older son once while flying but so far, their youngest was still fast asleep. They would really have to think of names for the boys, and soon.

Storm jumped out and moved around to where she was sitting. Georgia used one hand to unclip the belt. She carefully handed the baby to Storm before climbing out of the helicopter. He helped her take the final step down. Shale was already waiting, both babies now in his arms. He wore jeans and a t-shirt.

She turned, taking an immediate step back when a guy who looked very much like Shale walked up to them. He wore cotton yoga-style pants and was shirtless. His chest was covered in a golden marking. She looked from Shale to the guy. They were almost carbon copies. This was Shale's twin brother, for sure. "Oh, my fuck!" the Shale-look-alike bellowed. "It's true. It's fucking true!"

"Language, asshole," Shale boomed. "This is my brother, Sand. Sand, this is Georgia." Shale narrowed his eyes at his brother.

"So, you're the human who tamed this male." Sand pointed at Shale. "I'm looking at your whelps and I still can't believe it. When Granite told me about this I almost died. I think my heart stopped for a few seconds."

"You should stop being so damned dramatic." Shale looked angry. "In fact, you should just stop talking, period."

"Are you kidding me? Mister I'm-never-settling-down. Mister I-don't-want-kids. Really? Look at you." Sand was grinning broadly.

"Things change," Shale growled, jostling one of the babies into a better position. "Now shut the fuck up."

Sand held both hands up. "I had to come and see for myself, that's all! You can't blame me." He held a hand out to her. "It's lovely to meet you, by the way. I can see why my brother decided to—"

"Stop, Sand! Please." Shale implored him with his eyes.

Georgia felt her cheeks heat. Sand had this completely

wrong. She took his hand anyway. "Good to meet you."

"We need to get the babies inside and settled," Shale grumbled, walking towards large double doors.

"He's touchy, isn't he?" Sand grinned at her. "For the record, if he doesn't take care of you, you know where to find me." He winked at her. "I'll teach him." They were all walking, following Shale.

Georgia had to giggle. She couldn't help herself.

A scowling Shale turned back. "You can't kick my ass," he growled. "We've established that fact already." He kept walking, placing a hand on the doorknob.

"Kick your ass? Who said anything about kicking your ass? I happen to know you like this look, Georgie." Sand gestured to himself and winked at her. "I'll take your female from you if you can't take excellent care of her. We do have similar taste in females." He gave her an appreciative glance.

Shale growled low and deep. It was ten times worse than the growl he had given the paramedic. It sounded like a lion or a tiger or something. He threw the door open, turning to face them. "It's Georgia, not Georgie. We're parents to the twins but we're not together as a couple."

"Great!" Sand rubbed his hands together. "Then you won't mind if I ask Georgie here on a date."

"That would be a little weird, baby brother, don't you think? It's Georgia with an 'a.'"

Georgia wanted the ground to open up. She wanted someone to hose her down, her cheeks felt that hot. She also felt something else… not sorrow. Disappointment, maybe? She had somehow hoped that she and Shale might at least try at a relationship. Then again, he had given no indication it would ever happen.

"Baby brother?" Sand made a face of annoyance. "*Baby!* You're five minutes older. Five damned measly minutes."

They all walked inside. *Shit!* There were so many people in the large hall. Everyone was standing silent, listening in to the conversation that had just taken place. There were mostly men present. Lots and lots of men. All dressed in the same attire as Sand. Most had silver chests. There were also a few women. They were definitely dragon shifters. All of them were very tall and toned. They all wore short dresses and were quite attractive. The most beautiful of the bunch had dark hair and the bluest eyes Georgia had ever seen. She narrowed those eyes at Georgia and then smiled. There was nothing nice about the smile. It was more of a smirk. A self-satisfied smirk.

Who was she? Unfortunately, Georgia could guess. Shale had brought her there because he was trying to do the right thing. She needed to put aside any thoughts of the two of them getting together. Georgia was going to get hurt otherwise.

Shale was going to have to have a serious conversation with his asshole brother. *What the fuck!* Making moves on Georgia not even two minutes after they arrived on dragon soil. That was a new record low for the male. To make matters worse, he'd forced Shale to announce to half of his people that he and Georgia weren't together. Which was true. For now. It didn't mean that he didn't want to explore the possibility. She was the mother of his whelps. She was also kind and sweet. His mind turned to Georgia's mother. It took a special person to be willing to sacrifice so much for someone else. Georgia worked hard and not for herself. Never for herself. That much was apparent. He wasn't an idiot. He'd seen her ill-fitting clothing. Her purse was scuffed, as were her shoes. This was a female who thought about others first. Someone who was worried about taking a handout from him. On top of all of that, she was fucking gorgeous. Those eyes, that hair. Her body ripe and lush after bearing new life. If Sand came anywhere near this female, he was going to hurt his twin. If *any* male came near her, he was going to have to hurt them. He needed to play it cool, for now, since he didn't want to scare her. Things needed to progress slowly. One step at a time. Georgia was timid. This was a lot for a person to absorb.

He watched her now, taking in the lair as they walked to his chamber. Her eyes full of wonder. Every now and then she would gasp or touch a piece of furniture as they walked past. "It's beautiful." She turned back to him. "When you said 'lair'…" She shook her head, smiling.

"You thought hole in the ground and yet you came anyway?"

She shrugged. "Not a hole in the ground," she chided. "You have to admit that lair sounds… basic, but I don't mind basic, or old, or functional. I… guess I'm used to it." Shale had never really taken note of where he lived before. The lair was the lair. Seeing it through her eyes, however… it gave him a sense of wonder as well. The views were breathtaking. The lair itself was vast, light and airy. It was sparsely but beautifully furnished.

"Are those…? No…" She shook her head, pointing at one of the chandeliers. "I've seen a lot of what looks like…" she shook her head again, "can't be." Her brow furrowed.

"It's what we do," he said as they arrived at his chamber. "We mine," he added. "I run one of our mines… I *usually* run one of our mines. I've taken some time off."

"Dragons are into mining?" Her eyes were wide.

"Our lands are mineral-rich. We mine gold, platinum, diamonds… most of the precious and semi-precious stones."

"So," she touched the emerald-encrusted doorknob, "these are real?" She looked back up at the chandelier. "And those are too? Shit! They look like actual diamonds."

He nodded. "That's because they are. We sell limited stock to the humans, thus preventing the market from becoming flooded. If something is in demand it can fetch a higher price and will be more sought-after. So, you see, you do not need to work. Unless, of course, at some stage you would like to do something to contribute to our community."

"Well, we'll see. It's just so… unbelievable."

Shale grinned. "So you keep saying."

"Do you blame me?" She smiled back. "Up until a few hours ago, I didn't even believe in the existence of dragons and now… here I am."

"Here you are. This is my chamber." He nodded towards the door. "Can you open it for us?"

"Oh, of course." She pushed the door open and entered. "This is incredible!" She covered her mouth with her hands and turned a full circle. "It doesn't look masculine. I would have expected a bachelor pad."

"Actually… this isn't my place. It is now… It's ours, but it wasn't where I stayed before." His chamber had been somewhat of a bachelor pad. His old place had been smaller. Tiny kitchen. No bathtub. His room was in a loft that overlooked a well-appointed entertainment area.

"That explains it then." She laughed.

Shale noted that Georgia really didn't have a high opinion of him. "This apartment has three bedrooms. So enough for all of us. Each bedroom has its own bathroom en suite."

"That kitchen is amazing. Those countertops are white. That oven is huge."

"Earth dragons tend to have bigger families. Dragons have healthy appetites, especially growing boys."

"That makes sense."

"Let me go and put the babies down," Shale said. "Do you want to come and have a look."

"There's more?" She widened her eyes.

Shale nodded. "There most certainly is." He led the way, ignoring the first room, which he thought he would possibly take for himself. He walked into the second bedroom.

He smiled when he heard her gasp. "Oh, my goodness. Who did all of this?"

"Believe it or not, it was Sand. He had some help, of course. My brothers' mates, Louise and Breeze, helped out plenty."

"All of this in just a matter of hours?"

"Um… I contacted Sand as soon as you left last night."

Her eyes took on a shocked look. "*Then* already? You had no idea—"

"I knew the babies were due to be born any day. I knew they were mine. I hoped I could convince you to come back with me. Sand was on the phone early this morning.

He had to make things happen as soon as you went into labor." It was amazing what money could do. How quickly something could happen when you started throwing it around.

"I still can't believe all of this." She walked around the room. There were two cribs, she touched the cotton edging as she walked by. There was also a changing station. A rocking chair in the corner. The room was decorated in predominately white, with hints of mint green and brown. Shale put each baby down in his own crib. "You'll have to do the finishing touches yourself." He spoke softly. Not wanting to wake the boys. "A picture or two for the walls, a rug, one of those cute lamps." He shrugged. "There isn't too much in the way of clothing, enough to last the next couple of days…"

Georgia turned to him, her eyes shimmering with unshed tears. And she was smiling. She quickly closed the distance between them and threw her arms around him.

It was so unexpected that for a few seconds, he just stood there like an idiot.

"Thank you," she murmured into his chest.

By the time Shale had the common sense to put a hand up to her back, someone knocked on the door. Georgia pulled away. "This is amazing," she whispered.

"I haven't done much."

"You have!"

The knock sounded again. Harder this time. "There's someone at the door."

"Oh." She looked in the general direction of the living room. "You definitely have better hearing than me."

"Let's go and see who it is, unless you want to freshen up or something? In which case, I'll show you the bedroom choices and you can let me know which you would prefer. I put the twins in the middle, so either of us can get up during the night." They made their way back through to the living room area.

"I'm fine, and that sounds like a plan." Her eyes were wide with excitement.

Shale opened the door, surprised to see one of the healers on the other side. "Good evening, sire." She gave a small curtsey. "So, this is your human?" She curtseyed for Georgia as well, who looked amused.

"My name is Amethyst."

"Must be because of your beautiful eyes," Georgia remarked.

"Indeed." The female smiled broadly, giving a single nod of the head. "I have come to check on you and the whelps. I am told that the three of you are doing well? May I come in, my prince?"

Georgia squeezed her eyes shut for a second or two, clearly in disbelief. She was still struggling with the whole thing, but in a good way. Shale found her reactions adorable.

He moved to the side and the healer entered. "Let's go and take a seat over there." Amethyst gestured to the seating area. She was a typical elder, quick to give respect but just as quick to demand it right back.

"Can I offer you some tea?" Shale asked. "I'm sure there will be several kinds to choose from."

"No thank you, sire." She smiled. "I am sure you are eager to have me out of your hair."

"Not at all." Georgia shook her head. She and the healer sat next to each other on the couch. Shale chose the wingback chair opposite them.

"How are you feeling, child?" the healer asked Georgia.

"Surprisingly good actually, considering I pushed two babies out earlier today." She giggled in disbelief, putting a hand over her mouth.

Amethyst nodded. "It's great having improved healing capabilities. Of course, they're nowhere near as good as a shifter, but much better than a regular human. Okay, so no pains? Fever? Dizziness? I have to ask, just to be sure."

"None of those things." Georgia smiled.

"Good. How is the nursing going?"

"Very well, actually. It's like they read the manual or something, because I didn't. Those babies know exactly what to do."

"The rule of thumb is, if it hurts, you're doing it wrong. The babies should be fully latched onto the nipples. How many times have you fed them?"

"Our older baby three times now and the younger one only twice. I'm sure he'll be needing a feed soon."

"Don't let them sleep for longer than five hours. Wake them up if need be. Set an alarm if you have to. Newborns are sometimes sleepy. It can take a couple of weeks for them to wake up… so to speak. What about your breasts?"

Oh, fuck! This conversation was wandering into territories he didn't feel comfortable with. Georgia had great breasts before. They'd gone from great to phenomenal. Sure, he was probably a dick for noticing, but what could he say, he wasn't blind. He was also very much a male. *Stay cool! Stay calm! It wasn't a big deal.*

"What about them?" Georgia cupped her tits. Cupped them. Both hands. She squeezed. *Squeezed!*

Fuck!

Shale was thankful he still wore the jeans and t-shirt.

The jeans held shit together. He wanted to reposition himself right then but refrained. He was going to hell for his thoughts right now. Thoughts that involved his mouth on those soft mounds. *Fuck!* He needed to think about something else. Anything else.

"Any extreme sensitivity? Any pain?"

Georgia shook her head.

"Has your milk descended?"

"My milk what?" Georgia narrowed her eyes in contemplation. "Um… I… um… I don't think so."

"Are they hard or soft? Is one bigger than the other?"

"No, they're bigger than they normally would be." She cleared her throat. "I went up two cup sizes during the pregnancy."

Shit! He needed to move. His dick was right up against his zipper. It hurt! Instead, he leaned forward slightly, putting his elbows on his thighs, all nonchalant. Like hell that was how he felt.

"Do you know what to do when your milk descends? They might get really hard and achy."

"No, I've never heard of that." Georgia looked a little freaked out.

"It's nothing to be worried about. Unbutton your blouse, I'd like to examine you. It will be easier to explain."

"Um… o-okay, I guess that's alright." She giggled. "I've breastfed quite a few times so…" She looked pointedly at Shale.

Georgia began unbuttoning her blouse. *Fuck! Holy shit!* He needed to get out of there. Shale was a perverted fuck. That much was glaringly clear to him. He had to get out of there really badly, because he wanted to stay. He wanted to not only stay but he wanted to watch. He wanted to lean in and soak up her nude chest.

"I'm going to…" he cleared his throat, "get some tea. Can I make some for you ladies?"

"Actually," Georgia said as she pulled her blouse open, "I would love a cup. Herbal, if there is any."

Fuck!

He was going to hell. Straight to hell. That was all. She wore one of those feeding bras. He'd bought her a couple of things in the hospital and this was one of them. It was plain white cotton and, essentially, ugly as fuck. Yet somehow, it only made her tits look better because of it. Her nipples were huge. They pointed right at him accusingly. Like they knew what a sick fuck he was. The fabric strained to contain all of that loveliness. He wanted to groan out loud.

"No thank you, sire," the healer said, reminding him that she was there.

Shale managed to tear his gaze off her breasts and headed for the kitchen. He put the kettle on and grabbed some tits—teabags.

Fuck!

His gaze had drifted back to where the females were talking, and he caught sight of her breasts. Naked. Her bra was undone. They were full. Oh, so very lush. Her nipples were darker than he remembered them being – and he did remember them. He remembered everything about her naked form.

The healer was talking about milking Georgia manually if her mammary glands became overly full with milk. *What?* Even that sounded… better than it should. "The prince can always suckle you as well," the healer remarked. "Our males have been known to enjoy…"

He turned his attention back to the tea-making. Shale hadn't been able to help but notice how red her face had become. So much so that it bled down her neck and onto her chest. *That glorious chest.*

Shale put teabags into cups and added the boiling water. He put some honey onto the tray, taking a peek at the females, his heart in his fucking throat. His balls felt like they were there as well. He heaved out a sigh when he saw Georgia do up her blouse.

Shale plastered a smile on his face and headed back over. He placed the tray on the coffee table. His dick was going to have a red indent from the zipper. Thankfully it started calming down.

"You can go ahead and rut." She looked his way as she spoke.

Shale dropped the spoon he had just picked up. So much for his dick calming down. The fucker took note. Blood rushed south. *Rut! Hell yes!* He was all in!

"Rut?" Georgia looked confused.

"Sex, dear." The healer smiled. "It's good for you. Good for relaxation. Good for the two of you as a couple. Endorphins will be passed on to the babies through your milk." Amethyst obviously didn't notice how awkward things had become, because she went on. "I would recommend that you take it easy for the next few days. Don't overdo it." She looked pointedly at Shale and then at Georgia, whose eyes were as big as saucers. "Dragon shifters have very healthy appetites, but you'll know that already." She laughed. "Don't be afraid to tell him no if you're tired."

Georgia nodded slowly, looking like she was in a state of shock. Her throat worked. She not only looked unsure, but she looked a little… afraid. *No rutting then!*

"I'll leave the two of you to enjoy your tea and I'll get out of your hair. I'll be back in a day or two to check in on you. Don't hesitate to contact me if you're unsure of anything."

"Okay." Georgia smiled too brightly and nodded too vigorously.

"I'll see you out," Shale's voice was far too deep. He tried clearing his throat.

When he returned moments later, Georgia was clutching her mug tightly in both hands. "Thanks for this."

"Sure thing." He nodded, squeezing the back of his neck. "Um…"

"About…" They both started talking at once.

They laughed. Both of them sounded nervous as hell. *Was it a good thing?* Was Georgia nervous because something the healer had just said had struck a cord? He couldn't scent arousal. Then again, females were different to males, they didn't become aroused as easily. Or did they? It was like he didn't understand females anymore. Like he had zero knowledge of them. The thing was, he didn't. Not really. He was completely out of his depth.

"We should talk about what Amethyst just said," he tried again.

She nodded. "I guess we should."

Shale took a seat, choosing the wingback again. He picked up his mug.

"Not just Amethyst. Sand as well."

"I'm sure loads of assumptions are going to be made. It's important that we not listen to what anyone else has to say." He was about to tell her that no one else but them mattered. How they felt about each other or didn't feel about each other was no one's business but theirs. He was going to tell her that they should take it day by day. See where things went. He hadn't planned on pushing hard. He did want to plant a seed, though.

That when one of the babies yelled. It was loud.

"Okay." Georgia put her mug down. "It looks like one of the boys is hungry."

"Um, yeah," he said. "I'll go and fetch him and…"

"Look, don't worry about what everyone is assuming. I'm not worried in the least." She shrugged, looking like she meant it. "They'll soon realize that it's not like that between us."

What?

That was the last thing he had expected to hear.

"We're parents to those boys in there." She smiled, completely relaxed. "But we're not together. They'll get over themselves soon enough. You said it earlier. They just need to realize it."

"Yep… you're right," he muttered.

No.

Noooo!

There was another yell, it was followed by a wail. "I'd better get those hungry boys."

Georgia nodded and began to unbutton her blouse.

CHAPTER 18

Two days later…

Georgia felt warm and… Something niggled in her mind. She was too tired to try to focus on what that was. She didn't want to wake up. Was far too tired. Exhausted was a better description. She settled against… warmth. Georgia pulled in a deep breath. He smelled nice as well.

He.

Warm.

Nice smell.

She forced her eyes open, which was hard since they felt like someone had glued them shut.

"You should sleep." His voice was a deep baritone. His chest vibrated against her.

Georgia was in Shale's arms, against his chest. Snuggled in on the couch. She quickly sat up and scooched away.

"I'm sorry." Her voice was croaky. She felt groggy and was struggling to remember how she'd gotten there in the first place.

"I mean it, you really should sleep." He looked concerned. He also looked gorgeous. Who knew yoga-style pants could look so good on a man? Then again, Shale was seriously well-built. His chest and arms were things of beauty. The pants he had on were a deep blue and somehow accentuated his eyes. Okay, so it would seem that despite being half-dead, or at least feeling that way, she still found him attractive. *How was that even possible?*

Georgia looked down at herself. She still wore her pajamas. There was a splotch of dried up milk-vomit on her top. She touched her hair and... yeah... it was all scrunched up on the side she had been lying on. She knew she must look like complete shit. Her body ached from being so tired. "I need to shower," she mumbled.

"You need sleep," he reiterated.

"I need..." She smelled herself, getting hints of sour milk and BO. To think she'd been lying half on top of Shale. "I need a quick shower and then I'll call Macy to find out how my mom is doing. Then I'll climb into bed and try to get some more shut-eye. How long was I out for?" Not long enough, by how scratchy her eyes felt. The last she could remember, she'd been feeding one of the boys and then... nothing, which meant that Shale had put their son to bed and... She looked down, noticing that her feeding-bra had been clipped back up and the buttons on her top done up. Her cheeks heated. Shale must have fixed her clothing.

"About forty minutes." He scratched his head, then

yawned, putting a hand over his mouth. "Not long enough. Sorry about that... just now. I thought I'd sit down for a few minutes after putting the little one to bed and must have passed out as well. We're both just that tired."

"It's fine." She stood up. "Let me..." She scratched the back of her head, feeling a yawn building.

There was a demanding yell from the boys' room. Georgia sat back down, flopping back against the couch. She groaned. *No! Not so soon.*

"I'll go get him before he wakes his brother." Shale stood up.

She nodded, yawning. This was how it had been since coming home. *Home?* Did she already think of this place as home? That was the thing, it was home to her boys. They couldn't be out there in normal society, which meant that her home was here with them.

There was another almighty yell. So much for that healer advising them to wake the boys up every five hours. They were waking up every three hours, on average. Sometimes more often. It was a killer.

Shale walked back in, carrying the little one, who was calm against his daddy's wide chest. The baby was tiny in Shale's big hands. Right then, bare-chested with a baby, he could be on any calendar. Forget puppies, women everywhere would lap this up. Even Georgia, in her exhausted state, took notice.

The baby made a little gurgling noise. Georgia couldn't help but smile. It didn't matter how tired she felt.

"You go and take that shower," he urged. "We'll hang out for a bit. Hey, my boy?" His voice changed as he spoke to their son.

"You're sure? What if he starts to fuss?"

"I'll cope. We'll manage, baby, yes we will." He bounced their son a little. Again, his voice softened and became higher pitched as he spoke to their boy.

"Okay. I'll be as quick as I can. Knock on the door if he starts to fuss." Georgia hurried to her bedroom, passing the nursery as she did. She quickly grabbed fresh clothing, shaking her head all over again at the array of apparel in the closet. Most of the items fit too.

Georgia started the shower and quickly undressed, wrinkling her nose at the creased, puked on pajamas. They should probably be burned, they were that bad. She caught a glimpse of herself in the mirror and groaned. Her hair was a wild mess and, indeed, scrunched up on the one side. Her eyes looked hollow, and already dark smudges were making an appearance under her eyes. Her boobs were ginormous. They were so big that they made the rest of her look small, which was not the case. She hadn't been small before, not by a long damned shot. She was packing a few extra pounds after the pregnancy as well, so she was far from small now. Those boobs, though. Georgia shook her head. She needed to de-hair and exfoliate herself at some point. Maybe cut her rat's nest of hair.

Then she yawned again. *Yeah, all of that could wait.* She was so pooped, she wasn't sure why she was having such stupid ideas. Her only thoughts should be of her sons and of sleep, and in that order. She shouldn't be thinking about how she looked. Why on earth…?

Shale.

That's why. It was him. Georgia squeezed some toothpaste onto her toothbrush. She couldn't remember when she'd last brushed them. Yup, she had better things to do than think about Shale. She really needed to stop checking him out. She needed to be more careful about where she slept, and about straightening her own clothing as well. They'd had sex once. Just once. It was a while ago. It was over! It wasn't happening again! The last thing she wanted was for Shale to show interest because he felt obliged to do so. That would be awful. He had made it clear that he wasn't interested in her in that way. He had been nothing but kind, sweet and helpful since coming back in her life.

Sweet.

Kind.

Nope, he had no feelings for her. He may have been attracted to her once, but not anymore. Georgia turned to look at a side profile of herself. Her ass was bigger. Her hips were… *Arghhhhh!* Her boobs were worse. Oh, heaven help her. They were like big melons. Big, milk-filled melons. They were awful! She was hairy and—

Enough!

Georgia realized that she was being too hard on herself. She'd given birth just two days before. It felt like weeks. She smiled to herself. She was a mom. Her boys were healthy and beautiful. She was being an idiot. She stepped under the hot spray and groaned. She needed to concentrate on being a good mother. That was all! She also needed to check in with Macy. She hoped her mom was doing okay. Georgia put the toothbrush down on the rack and lathered up. She put shampoo in her hair and rinsed off, feeling some of the tension in her shoulders release. She put a detangling conditioner in her hair and brushed her teeth before doing a final rinse and stepping out of the shower.

Georgia quickly toweled off and got dressed. It felt like she'd been gone for ages. She already felt so much better. It was amazing what a freshen up could do for a person.

She contemplated leaving her hair as it was. It would be a wild mess if she did that. Georgia massaged a no-rinse conditioner into her wet locks and brushed it through. She considered putting on a little make-up. *No! Not happening!* Georgia quickly made her way back to the living room.

She could hear the baby fussing. *Damn!* She'd taken too long. She should have just left her hair. Then she heard Shale sing. *No freaking fair.* The guy had a good voice as well. A body like a warrior god, the face of an angel... *Were there male angels?* It didn't matter. He looked like one and sounded like one too. He sang a nursery rhyme but made up his own words. It was too cute.

Georgia looked around the door jamb, noting that Shale faced the other way. He was bouncing lightly on the balls of his feet, rocking the baby, still singing.

The baby's fussing grew louder and angrier. He was hungry. She had already come to recognize that particular cry.

Her breasts felt full and tight. Her nipples tingled. "Let me take him," she said, walking into the room.

Shale turned and smiled. "You look better."

"I feel better. Thank you."

"I changed his diaper," Shale said as the little one gave a loud wail.

Her breasts tingled some more. "I think you'd better give him to me."

Shale was staring at her chest.

"What is it?" She looked down. "Oh shit! You'd better give him to me quickly." There were wet spots on her top.

One on each breast. The spots were getting bigger and bigger with every passing second. Her boobs still felt tight. Her nipples were tingling even more. The baby was full-on crying now and her body was reacting.

Georgia sat down. By now, her top was plastered to her chest and very wet. How much freaking milk was even inside her? This was ridiculous. "Give him to me," she half-yelled.

When she looked up, Shale was grinning. He was looking at her chest and grinning. Then he was chuckling. "A different type of wet t-shirt contest, Wyoming, and I have to say, you win!" She could tell that he was joking. "You're the hands-down winner!" His eyes were still on her boobs.

Georgia found herself smiling. "I'm the only person in this competition, so it stands to reason I would win."

She pulled her soaking top open. It was one of those numbers specially designed for breastfeeding. Then she unclipped her wet bra and held her hands up for her son, who was still crying. Milk still leaked from her nipples. It was a mess.

"Um… I'm pretty sure you'd win in a room full of contestants, Georgia." Was it her imagination or had Shale's voice sounded husky just then? What was that look in his eyes? It wasn't lust. *No damned way!*

She looked back down at her now squirting boob, quickly putting her son to her nipple. He latched beautifully.

"I'll go and get you something to help clean up with," Shale said as he walked from the room.

Um… nope, there was no way he had been checking her leaky, sticky, milky breasts out. There was just no way.

Shale reappeared moments later, carrying a towel. "I wasn't sure whether to get you clean clothing." He winced. "I didn't want to rifle through your underwear drawer."

"That'll work."

CHAPTER 19

She smiled up at him as he placed the towel on the sofa next to her, within reaching distance.

"I could help you... dry up." *Wipe her breasts.* Was he seriously offering to wipe her chest for her?

"I'm good." She smiled. "I'll get to it in a moment. This little guy is already getting sleepy."

"Milk drunk," Shale said, watching his son feeding. *Lucky little tyke.*

Not looking.

Not thinking about Georgia's breasts.

Not doing it!

His dick was taking notice though. It shouldn't, and again, it may make him a sicko, but there it was. Who made feeding clothing white? That was insane. He swallowed thickly, recalling how she had looked with her top plastered to her chest. Her plump nipples poking holes through the cotton fabric. Her mounds full. So gloriously full.

He leaned forward, resting on his elbows hoping she didn't notice that he was sporting a semi, and if he didn't think about something else, he would have a full-blown erection soon. "We need to come up with names for these boys."

"I know." She pushed out a breath. "It's a tough one. My brain feels foggy. Naming a child is such an important thing. They have to live with whatever name their parents give them for the rest of their lives."

"We have to start somewhere. Did you have something in mind?" he asked. "What about your dad?"

Shale assumed the male had passed away. Might be nice to—

"No way!" She shook her head, her shoulders tensing. Her eyes held a look of horror.

"Oh, I just assumed he was dead and that—"

"He left my mom and me when I was eight. He came home one day and packed his stuff up. My dad told us that he was done with the rat race. With the nine-to-five drone. He was done with being responsible. Raising a kid apparently wasn't for him. My mom tried to talk him into staying. I just remember crying and crying. I loved my dad." She shrugged. "I didn't want him to go. Then he up and left, and that was the last I saw of him."

"What is his name?" Shale asked.

"Patrick."

"Okay, so definitely not Patrick then. I'm sorry you had such a bad experience." It was such a lame-ass thing to say. It would have been a defining moment in her life. No wonder she had expected him to be a deadbeat. *No fucking wonder.* Shale ground his teeth together for a moment.

"Guy was a real winner!" he added, feeling pissed off.

"We were okay after he left." Georgia put their son on her shoulder and tapped his back softly. "My mom had to work two jobs after that. I got a part-time job as soon as I was able. We had each other." Her voice hitched. He watched the column of her throat work. "Now you understand why I can't abandon her."

"I completely understand," Shale said. "I'm working on it. I don't want to say too much because I don't want to get your hopes up. There is a plan in motion."

The baby burped. It was soft and at just the right moment. They locked eyes and laughed. "Thank you," she murmured when the moment ended. "I appreciate it. I appreciate everything you've done for us. It's more than I could ever have imagined." She looked like she was struggling with something. "My dad left because we were cramping his style. We were making him feel claustrophobic. I don't want you to ever feel that way."

What the fuck? Was she really comparing him to her deadbeat asshole of a father? Shale forced himself to hear her out.

"We're sharing this apartment right now, but we don't have to keep this living arrangement. It might be a bit awkward when you date other people. When we both… date… other, um, people."

What the hell?

"I mean you can, that is, date other people. I don't want to get in your way. If that's what you want, then…" She shrugged. "You're a fantastic father. I would never deny you your sons. I just wanted you to know that."

"Good to know." He nodded once, his mind racing. *What was she saying?* His blood boiled at the thought of her with other males. "Your dad left because he was an asshole. He made a ton of excuses. None of them were valid. You and the boys will never cramp my style."

She nodded. "Good. I'm glad. You can date, though, and we don't have to always live together."

"I'm going to assume you don't plan on dating anyone just yet?" He fucking prayed that wasn't the case. "I mean you just gave birth and you're, well…" He pointed at her wet shirt.

"No!" She choked out a laugh. "Of course not! I have no plans on dating anyone any time soon. That's for sure. I have my hands full." She looked down at their son, her eyes filling with warmth.

"So, let's not think about all that. We don't have to just yet. I hope I've made myself useful."

"Yes," she nodded, "I'm not sure what I would do if you weren't here."

"Good, so let's forget about separate apartments… at least for now." There was nowhere else he wanted to be.

She nodded. "Okay, that sounds like a plan."

The baby started fussing again. Georgia sighed. "Maybe he's still hungry." She opened up her top and put him back on her breast. The little one sucked like a mad thing.

"Do you want something to drink?"

There was a knock on the door. Shale frowned. "I'll go and see who that is. Might be one of my brothers, or one of their mates coming to check on us. They will be wanting to meet the boys. Shall I send them away? They've called quite a few times, and I keep putting them off."

She looked worried for a second or two and then shook her head. "It's fine. It would be nice to meet your family. At least I'm showered. Who knows when that will be the case again?" She laughed.

"Okay, then." Shale went to the door as whoever it was knocked again.

Great! He let everyone in. "This is my oldest brother, Granite, and his mate, Louise."

"Hi." Louise waved. "It's so lovely to finally meet you."

"Louise is also a human," Shale added.

"You already know my brother, Sand."

"Hi," Georgia said, looking a little shell-shocked.

"Where are my nephews?" Shale asked Louise.

"We thought we'd leave them at home. We're here for a very quick visit. We wanted to meet you guys. We didn't want to bombard you." She giggled.

When Shale glanced Sand's way, he noticed his brother's eyes were practically glued to Georgia's chest. *Fucker!* "You do realize your shirt is wet, Georgia," Sand piped up, a grin about a mile wide on his asshole of a face. He was totally ogling Georgia's tits. *What the fuck was wrong with the male?*

Shale growled, clenching his fists. He wanted to punch the little shit in the jaw.

"Chill!" Sand held up both hands. "I was just letting Georgia know." He shrugged like it was no big deal, looking back down at her chest.

Georgia made a little squeaking noise and reached for the towel. "I had forgotten about that."

"Let me help you." Shale picked it up before she could reach it. He opened the towel, using it to cover Georgia. He even pulled it a little over her breast and the feeding baby. "Can I get you one of those woolen blankets?" he asked, raising his brows.

"This is fine." Georgia nodded. "Thanks."

"No problem." His smile quickly turned into a scowl as his gaze lifted to Sand. Shale stared daggers at his brother. The male ignored him flat.

"Have you guys decided on names yet?" Granite asked.

Georgia shook her head. "No, not yet. It's tough trying to choose."

"For now, it's Twin-1 and Twin-2, I'm assuming." Louise smiled broadly.

"Something like that." Shale had to smile back, even though he was still feeling pissy with his brother. "It's that or the older baby or younger baby. Neither works very well."

"I can imagine," Granite chuckled. "Do you want some help? What about Chalk, or Slate?"

"Chalk?" Georgia looked horrified. "Slate's okay."

"Then there's Basalt or…"

"As Earth dragons, we like to name our offspring after rock or land features like Mountain or Rock or…" Granite went on.

"I had noticed, but Chalk?" Georgia smiled. She had a great smile. Her eyes brightened.

"Where is Baby-2?" Louise asked.

"You mean Baby-1? Since this is Baby-2, if we're going to get technical," Georgia said, still smiling. She patted the little one's back. The towel had come down some, exposing the top part of her amazing-as-fuck breast.

Sand was practically drooling. He bit back a snarl. The male had absolutely no shame.

"He's sleeping," Georgia said.

"Here." Shale pulled the towel up a little, smiling at

Georgia, hoping to god she couldn't see how tense he was.

"Thanks."

"Sleeping?" Louise looked puzzled. "Why would he be sleeping?" she asked. "You do know that you need to get these two onto the same routine, don't you?"

"I've been reading the books and they suggest that we feed on demand, which seems right. If a baby is hungry, feed it and change it and burp it and change it again, if need be, before putting the little one down." Georgia pushed out a breath. "I must say, it is tough. No sooner is one baby down than the other is awake."

Louise laughed. "Oh, honey," she shook her head, "that might work with a singleton. It will never work with twins. You need a routine. You need to get them on the same routine. It needs to happen now. Wake the other one up. Go fetch him, Shale."

"It seems wrong!" Georgia looked worried. "We only got him down not so long ago."

"I know what I'm talking about. Either you're waking them, or they'll be waking you. Excuse me saying this, but you both already look shattered. Give it another few days and you'll be..." She laughed. "I don't want to even think about how exhausted you'll be."

"Louise has experience," Shale said. "She's had two sets of twins."

"Two?" Georgia's eyes nearly popped out of her skull.

Shale chuckled. *Fuck, but she was adorable.* She looked his way. "You'd better go wake up One."

"I'll put Two down." Shale reached down and took the baby from her.

"You'd better give Two to me." Louise held her arms out. "I'm going to wake him up and tickle him and kiss him. I'm ultimately going to try to keep him awake until you're done with his brother. If you guys are strict about it, you'll have something of a life back in a day or two, once they're in a routine."

"Okay. You'll have to give me more tips please."

Louise blew raspberries on the baby's tummy. "Don't get any ideas, sweetheart, please." Granite scowled heavily as he watched his mate with the baby.

Louise laughed.

His family visited for about an hour. He was glad to see how well Georgia and Louise got along. Louise would be a big help to Georgia. It looked like the two of them could be friends even.

Shale saw them to the door. Granite put a hand on his arm. "You have a beautiful family."

Shale wanted to tell Granite that they weren't technically a family, but he held it back. He hoped it would be the case soon, despite how Georgia pushed him away. "Any news on that thing we discussed?"

Granite frowned. "Blaze isn't happy about it. We're still in discussion about the ins and outs of the whole thing."

"It's not an outright 'no' though?" Shale held his breath.

"No, but it could take some time before things are resolved."

"We don't have much time."

Granite pushed out a breath. "It's the best I can do right now. I'm working on it, I swear. Please sit tight for now."

"For now," Shale said, knowing that he couldn't keep Georgia from her mother for much longer. It wasn't safe out there. By now, word would have gotten out about the miracle twins with the strange chest markings.

Granite squeezed his arm, looking at him with concern. His brother nodded once.

Shale heard laughter behind him. He turned back, watching as Sand hugged his female. She nodded at something he had said and was smiling… broadly. "Thank you! You have no idea what a compliment like that means to me right now. I feel like a milk machine."

"Well, you look like a sex goddess," Sand went on.

Shale growled, his chest vibrated. In fact, it felt like the floor vibrated a little.

"Calm yourself down, brother," Sand snorted.

He noticed that both the babies had been left on the sofa. Cushions had been placed around them. "I'm worried about the babies," he outright lied. "They shouldn't be left alone like that."

"They're safe," Georgia stammered. "Babies don't have the physical strength to roll at this stage."

"They're not regular babies." He had a hard edge to his voice. Quite frankly he was smarting at how Sand was shamelessly flirting with Georgia, and how she was just lapping it up. Especially right after she had just pretty much told him she wanted to move out and date other people. *His brother, though? Fucking hell!* This was a mess.

"Still," Georgia walked back to the sofa, sitting on the edge, "I really don't think they…" Then she pushed out a breath. "You're right," she nodded, "I should never have left them like that." Her eyes welled a little, but she blinked twice and seemed to recover. "I'll be more careful. I would hate for something to happen…" Her eyes were wide and trained on the babies.

Shale felt like an asshole. Who was he kidding? He *was*

one. *Fuck!* This sucked. "No, you're right too. I think I overreacted." He raked a hand through his hair. "I'm sorry."

"No," she shook her head some more, "*you're* right!"

Her admission made him feel even worse. "I'll see you out." He clenched his jaw as his eyes landed on Sand. *Little shit!* He needed to grow the fuck up.

Sand grinned. "Bye, Georgia. For the record, I think you're doing an amazing job as a mom." He winked at her and Shale had the urge to tear the male's eye right out.

Shale gestured for the hallway. Once they reached the door, he followed Sand out. "You need to stay away from Georgia."

"Jealous much?" Sand smirked.

"No, this has nothing to do with jealousy. I know your type."

"My type?" Sand laughed.

"Yes, asshole." Shale fought at keeping his voice down. "Your type. All you want is a good time, and Georgia is not that kind of female."

"If you say so, bro." Sand chuckled.

"She's fucking not! I don't want to see you pulling moves on her. Are we clear?"

"Crystal." Sand held up his hands. "We're friends and I happen to like her a lot."

"You don't even know her, so you can stop with the bull already." He knew what Sand's idea of friendship was.

"You guys aren't dating or anything, right? I mean, that *is* what you said?"

"We're not together but I will be looking out for her." Shale narrowed his eyes on Sand.

"Not because you want her for yourself and you're jealous?" He raised his brows.

"No! I'm looking out for the mother of my children. Is that so difficult for you to understand?"

"Not at all." Sand looked like he was privy to some huge insider joke, which only incensed Shale more. "Um… you haven't forgotten about Breeze's birthday celebration tomorrow night, have you?"

Crap! He made a face. "I completely forgot about it, with everything going on."

"Breeze mentioned that she's excited to meet Georgia, but I'm sure she would understand if you can't make it though."

"Yeah, Breeze said the same to me when I saw her yesterday. I'm just so out of it I forgot completely." He raked a hand through his hair.

They said their goodbyes and Sand left. Georgia had just put the babies down for a nap when he returned. "I'm going to lie down for a while. Catch up on my reading." She held up one of the baby books. "I wish they had a book on raising dragons. It would help enormously."

Shale felt like a dick all over again. He squeezed the back of his neck. "You're doing a great job." It sounded hollow after what had happened.

She widened her eyes for a moment. "I'm trying. I really am."

He reached forward and took her hand. "You're doing a great job. I mean it."

She nodded once, holding up the book. "I really need to get some shut-eye. I hope this whole routine, 'wake the babies up' thing works." She yawned.

"One last thing." He sucked in a breath. "It's Breeze's

birthday tomorrow. She's having a celebration. A cocktail party or something. I completely forgot about it, even though Breeze reminded me yesterday. She really wants us to go. We can bring the boys. Having said that, she'll completely understand if we can't make it."

"You told me about them. That would be Granite's twin, Volcano, and his mate Breeze?"

"Yes." Shale nodded his head. "They have twin girls."

"I doubt we could go for long but I'm sure we could at least pop our heads in and wish her a happy birthday. Of course, you could stay longer if you wanted." She got a panicked look. "We don't have a gift!"

"Don't worry about that. I'll take care of it."

"You take care of everything." She gave him a smile. "Makes me feel bad sometimes.

"Don't! That's what I'm here for." He wished he was there for more, but he would take what he could get.

"You're sweet. Okay then, that sounds good." She nodded.

"It's a date then." He smiled at her.

Georgia laughed. "But not a *date* date." A statement. Not a question. In fact, by the way she laughed, she thought he was nuts for even suggesting it.

"Of course not!" he laughed back, feeling like shit.

CHAPTER 20

The next evening…

Georgia twisted her arm so that she could see the time on her watch. She was still in her robe. She'd managed to tame her hair and to apply most of her makeup. All she needed to do now was apply lipstick and slip on her dress. A long, black number Shale had conjured up out of nowhere. It had a zip up the front and the cut flattered her curves. There was also a velvet box on the table next to where the heels were. A simple pair of earrings, he'd said. Something to wear with the dress, he'd added. She wasn't sure what to make of it. *Nothing!* She finally decided. Absolutely nothing. The heels were low and black with silver details. They matched the dress beautifully.

Georgia was feeding the boys. Both of them at once. It was still a bit awkward, but she was getting the hang of it.

The key was to use pillows. Propping the boys up 'just so.' Once she was done, she was going to throw on her dress and they'd head to the party, which had already started. In fact, at this rate, by the time they got there, it would be an hour into the celebrations.

"Don't look so worried," Shale said, looking amazing. He wore a pair of black cotton pants and nothing else. His skin was bronzed and he had this five o'clock shadow on his jaw. How was it that when women didn't shave, they looked scruffy and unkempt, yet on a man, it was rugged and sexy? It wasn't fair. She'd barely managed to shave her legs and then only from below her knees down. There had been no time for more. She'd even nicked the side of her leg because she'd been in such a rush.

Yet, there he was looking rugged and seriously handsome. She suspected he'd look good in anything. Half-dressed, though… Georgia had to tear her eyes off his six-pack. "I'm not worried. I just don't like being late," she finally said, when she realized he was waiting for a reply. She was also worried about going to the party. About being there with Shale. They weren't together and it was awkward. People said things. They assumed things. It was all awkward, especially when she *did* have feelings for Shale. She *did* want this evening to be a *date* date. She'd said it the day before in the hopes he would agree, but nope. So, it would be stilted and uncomfortable. She'd end up having to correct people. Even worse, Shale would do it.

We're not together.
It's not like that.
We're not on a date *date.*
We're parents to these boys and that's it! Final!

It hurt.

"It can't be helped if we're a bit late," Shale said, taking her out of her thoughts. "Breeze doesn't mind. It's a casual evening," he added. "It's not like it's a sit-down dinner party or anything. Don't worry about it." He shrugged.

Casual. Right. Not hardly. That dress probably cost more than she made in a year. Georgia was nervous. She was too tired to pretend otherwise. Too damned tired, period.

"I packed a diaper bag." He held it up.

"Great." She smiled. She'd lucked out with Shale. Maybe a little too much, hence not being able to get him… or fantasies of them, out of her mind.

"The stroller is all set as well." He wheeled it closer to the sofa.

"These two are pretty much done drinking." She looked down at the boys who were sleeping on her breasts. Not great, according to the book she was reading. Babies should learn to self-soothe. They shouldn't be allowed to fall asleep drinking. It would apparently become a habit. Someone should have told the boys that. It was almost impossible to feed the twins without them falling asleep at the breast.

"They're so gorgeous," Shale's voice was husky. He reached down and picked up Two, putting him over his shoulder. He began patting his back softly. She did the same with One.

"Any ideas as to names yet?" she asked, grimacing. Soon, One and Two were going to stick. That could not be allowed to happen.

He sighed. "None." Shale wiped a hand over his jaw, the stubble catching. "We'll figure it out. I quite like the ring of One and Two." He grinned.

She laughed. "Don't be silly. We need to find names soon, because nicknames can stick."

"You're right about that, Texas." He winked at her.

Shale didn't joke about the name thing very often. Calling her by the different states made her think of their night together. She wondered if it made him think of their night too. It also made her want sex again. With Shale. It didn't matter how tired she was. How leaky her breasts were. None of that mattered. She needed to stop this line of thinking, since it wasn't going to happen. "At least if you get puked on you can just wipe it off." She tried at a silly joke, hoping he hadn't noticed how uncomfortable he had made her feel just by calling her Texas.

Shale barely cracked a smile. "I think he's fast asleep." He glanced at the baby in his arms.

"Yep," she whispered, looking down at the sleeping infant in her arms. "I think we're good." She closed her robe, holding back a yawn. Georgia was beyond tired. She envied her twins right then. Fast asleep, bellies full, no need for small talk.

Georgia watched Shale carefully lower the little one into one of the bassinets on the stroller. It was a really fancy pants stroller. It was made especially for twins and could be fitted with either bassinets or car seats.

Shale came over and picked up One, placing him in the lower of the two bassinets. "You go and get dressed and we can—"

Two gave a loud bellow. "Oh shoot," she said, making a face. "I guess he wasn't as sound asleep as you thought."

Shale frowned. He picked Two up. "Shit!" His frown grew. "I guess he must have had a burp inside him after all." He made a face.

Georgia got up and walked over. Two's one-piece had a wet, congealed milk spot all the way down the front. One thing she'd come to realize was that babies spat up milk regularly. Her hair or her top frequently had some vomit in or on it.

Two was squirming, his face was all scrunched up.

"I'll take care of it." She took Two from Shale. "You go."

One let out an almighty cry from inside the bassinet.

Shale groaned. "It's as if they know we have to be somewhere."

"Exactly." She laughed. What else was there to do in a situation like this. "They might sense our nerves…" *Oh shit!* She was nervous about being out with Shale. More so than she had realized. It had nothing to do with the babies, but she didn't want him to know that. "It'll be the first time we're out with the boys," she quickly added.

Shale nodded and picked up One, who was fussing in earnest by now.

"Let me go and change this little munchkin," Georgia said as she walked.

It was hard to believe, but she was already an expert after only a few days at this. His diaper was still fine, so she stripped him out of the one-piece, despite his protests. She'd read that babies, newborns in particular, didn't enjoy being naked, and boy, was it true. Dragon, human, it didn't matter, in this they were the same. She did up the last snap and picked Two up, giving him a cuddle. "It's okay." He calmed instantly. "I think you might need some more milk," she said, as they walked back to where Shale was waiting.

One was kicking his legs, making choked crying noises. Shale was doing his best to calm the little guy but failing dismally. The choked cries were growing louder by the second. He gave her a pained look. "Something tells me they didn't drink enough."

Georgia sat back down on the sofa, positioned the cushions and opened her robe. Two instantly calmed as he latched, while One's wails grew even louder and more demanding. Her boobs tingled. "Give him to me before there's milk everywhere."

Shale walked over, he handed their son to her. Georgia positioned him, and he latched too, sucking greedily. Exhaustion settled in. Days of broken sleep were starting to seriously take their toll. She was also worried about her mom. About her feelings for Shale and the fact that she shouldn't be feeling this way. She wasn't allowed to. Not when it wasn't reciprocated. It was a recipe for disaster. The boys were slowly getting into a routine, but it was taking time. Rome wasn't built in a day, and all that.

Shale sat back down. "Can I get you anything? Something to drink maybe?"

He was so darned polite. Too polite. She hated it. They worked well together as parents to these two little boys, but that's where it ended. She supposed it was enough. Georgia wanted more though. It would be better if they moved into separate apartments as soon as possible. It was driving her nuts.

Using her eyes, she pointed at the bottle of water next to her. "I'm all set. Why don't you head out?"

Shale shook his head. "Nah! I'll hang with you guys."

"Go!" she insisted. "It's a family celebration. You should be there."

"I can't just leave you here to—"

"Of course you can. I'm quite capable. I'm feeling really tired. I thought I'd cope okay but maybe it was a bit premature to be heading out. I'm going to try to get them down and then head to bed." She bit back another yawn.

Georgia was shocked at how disappointed he looked. It made her feel like maybe… maybe there was a chance for them. It lasted all of a few seconds though. "If you're sure?"

"I'm sure. You go and celebrate with your family. Tell Breeze how sorry I am that I can't make it."

"You're truly sure? I'll wait until they settle, and we can head there for half an hour. Everyone was looking forward to meeting the boys."

The real reason for his disappointment. "Go, Shale! No use both of us missing out." Georgia really didn't feel like attending the event. "I hope you don't mind." Now she was being too polite. It sucked.

"If you're sure," he repeated.

"Absolutely." She nodded.

"Okay then." He stood up. "I won't stay. I'll show my face. Hang out for a bit and then head back. Call me if you need anything." He patted his pocket. She assumed his cellphone was in there.

"I will." Georgia smiled. "We'll be fine. You go and have fun."

Shale nodded once and left. It didn't take long and the boys were sound asleep. Georgia put them in their beds and headed back into the living room. She couldn't resist. She opened the royal-blue, velvet box and almost fell on the floor. *Something small. This was something small?*

Georgia walked over to the wingback and sat down

heavily, the box still clutched in her hand. She unfolded the note inside.

> *Thank you for giving me the best gift*
> *imaginable.*
> *Always,*
> *Shale*

Inside the box was a pair of diamond earrings. They were heart-shaped and set in what had to be platinum, since shifters were allergic to silver. The box also held a necklace with two heart-shaped diamond pendants. She was sure that the hearts represented each of their sons. It was the word 'always' that gave her pause. *Always? What did that mean?*

One thing was for sure, Shale had gone to a ton of effort, and she'd just ditched him because she couldn't handle whatever was or wasn't going on between them. She needed to put on the dress and the jewelry. She needed to grow a pair and go and find out what 'always' meant. She needed to, at least, be honest about how she felt, even if Shale didn't feel the same.

Once she'd made the decision, her heart began to pound, and her palms felt sweaty. At the same time, she felt giddy with excitement. She clutched the jewelry to her chest. Moreover, she clutched that note to her chest. That simple piece of paper. It meant so much to her.

CHAPTER 21

Where is Georgia?
Where are the boys?

A question he'd heard half a dozen times since arriving at the function. Shale felt bad for leaving her. He was going to finish this drink and head home. Someone clapped him on the back. Shale turned, seeing Granite. His brother smiled. "How are you holding up?"

"Doing okay."

Granite cocked his head, scrutinizing him.

"It's tough, but I'm loving it." Shale opened up. "Georgia is great."

Granite raised his brows. "Where *is* your lovely female?"

"The boys were restless. She's tired. I think she might have been a little apprehensive about meeting the family. She's not my female, by the way. That might be part of the problem."

"Of course she's your female." Granite grinned, which was weird since his brother hardly ever smiled this broadly. The only time he ever saw softness in his expression or demeanor was when he was looking at his mate or his children. "I can see it by the way you look at one another."

"I'm not so sure."

"I am! You guys still need to figure it out. That's all." His brother gave him another clap on the back.

"Okay. If you say so." Shale wasn't sure what to say. "Listen," he looked the male head on, "any news on Georgia's mother? I'm sorry to have to push you for an answer but we're out of time. I need to fetch her mom tomorrow, or we need to head there for a day. I'd rather not risk my family."

"Your family?' Granite raised his brows.

"You know what I mean."

"Blaze is still on the fence. I have a feeling he's going to veto the whole thing."

Shale sucked in a breath, ready to argue. Blaze could piss him the fuck off.

"Take it easy," Granite said. "I'm going to make the decision for him. You can bring Georgia's mother back to our lair and implement the necessary, as discussed in our meeting."

"Are you serious? Won't you be in shit?"

Granite shrugged, narrowing his eyes. "You plan to go over our heads and bring her regardless, don't you?"

"Yep, you know me so well." Shale smiled. "There's no way I'm putting my family in jeopardy. Hunters could be all over Dalton Springs by now. They'll have Georgia's name and details. I can't send her back there."

"I'll take the fallout over this. Blaze will get over himself."

"Thank you!" He took his brother in a quick hug.

"Hopefully it gets you some brownie points and you can figure this thing out with Georgia."

"I sure hope so." Did she really feel that way about him? Was Granite right?

Shale needed to get back to his chamber. He needed to ask her straight out.

He downed the rest of his whiskey, the ice chinked against the side of his glass as he put it down on a nearby table. Shale turned, spotting Breeze on the far side of the room. She was dancing with Volcano; the two of them only had eyes for one another. He couldn't help but smile as he watched them for a moment or two. He decided to forgo saying goodbye, he was sure his brother's mate would understand him leaving. As he turned back, he collided with—"Topaz," he said, reaching out to grab her by the upper arms so that she didn't fall.

Shale held on to her for a second or two while she regained her footing, then let her go. The female didn't step back as he expected. He watched a sensual smile form on her lips. At least, up until a couple of months ago – six months and a handful of days, if he was going to be exact – he would have found her smile intoxicating.

Not anymore.

Her lips didn't have the pink color he'd come to fantasize about. He let his eyes drift over her face. Her skin was flawless... but he'd come to love a certain smattering of freckles. Topaz's smile grew. She obviously thought he was checking her out. She was a beautiful dragon. Males fell over their feet for her. She was wrong about him checking her out though. Very wrong. Topaz flicked her long, inky hair over her shoulder. She narrowed her beautiful blue eyes on him. *Blue.* Green had become a firm favorite. The green had to be a certain hue and definitely highlighted by a mane of fiery red hair. Otherwise, it just wouldn't do.

"So, you're a dad now?" Her voice was a soft purr. Her dress was short. An inch or two above mid-thigh. Her legs were long and toned. *Still nothing! Not a damn thing.* Not when he preferred soft and lush. Curves that went on for days. *Fuck!* He needed to get out of there. He hoped Georgia had opened the gift he had left her. He wondered what she thought of it. His heart beat a little faster at the thought.

"Um… Shale… did you hear what I said? I asked about your whelps." Topaz was frowning, aware of his distraction, even though he was looking directly at her.

"Yes," he muttered. "I'm a dad. They're…" He got what felt like a goofy smile. "I need to get back home to them."

"Oh, come on, Shale." She graced him with one of her sultry smiles. "You can't go quite so soon. I'm sure mom has everything under control. Did I hear right when you said that the two of you aren't together? You're raising the whelps together, but that's where it ends?"

Before he could answer, she moved closer, her chest brushing against his, making him feel seriously uncomfortable. "Does that mean we still get to fool around?" she purred. "It's been a long time, my prince. Too long." She wrapped a hand around his bicep.

Shale took a step back, breaking the contact. "You heard the ass-end of a conversation that was taken out of context." He tried not to snap at the female but failed. This felt like a slight to Georgia. Shale didn't like it one bit.

"Sounded pretty cut and dried to me." Topaz folded her arms.

"Well, it wasn't. It *isn't!* Georgia and I are very much together. Not just as parents to our whelps but as a couple." He hoped and prayed it would soon be true.

"A couple?" She raised her brows, her nostrils flaring. He could tell she didn't buy it. Not for a second.

"It's not any of your business, Topaz." He knew she could scent that they hadn't rutted. "My female recently gave birth."

"I see." She smiled. "You know where to find me if you change your mind."

"I won't."

"She's not your type at all, you know," Topaz snapped. She made a face like Georgia was somehow beneath him.

"You're right, Topaz." He smiled. "You're so damned right. I don't normally go for sweet, kind or funny. I don't normally go for a female who always puts others before herself..." He shook his head. "I never had a female like that in my life before. Someone selfless and... did I mention kind? I think I did, but it's worth mentioning again. Then there's fucking gorgeous as well. Gorgeous with just the right amount of sass to round it all off. Now that I've been lucky enough to find a female of Georgia's caliber, I'm afraid there is no going back."

Topaz's mouth had dropped open. Her eyes were wide. He didn't stay to see what her reaction would be. Quite frankly, he didn't care.

Shale walked out into the hallway... and *her* scent hit

his nostrils. Coconut with a fruity edge. "Georgia." He caught the faint scent of his whelps as well. *What?* Shale looked up and down the hallway. He went back inside to where the function was taking place, scanning the area. There was no sign of Georgia. Her scent disappeared as he walked further inside. He stepped back into the hallway.

"Are you looking for your female?" One of Granite's guards stood outside.

"Yes, have you seen her?"

"Yes," he nodded, "she left with your brother, Sand, a couple of minutes ago. I don't want to get in the middle of this, but… you should know…" He shook his head. "Don't worry about it. They headed that way." *Probably on their way to Sand's chamber. What the fuck!*

"What were you going to say?" He narrowed his eyes on the male.

The male shook his head. "I don't want to make trouble."

"Spit it out," Shale growled.

"Your brother had his arm around your female. He was pushing the stroller. I thought it a little strange." The male shook his head. "It was probably nothing."

CHAPTER 22

The babies were sound asleep in the stroller. They hadn't been fed that long ago, so she probably had at least two, if not three hours before they stirred again. She touched the pendants at the base of her neck, then smoothed her dress. It was a tight fit over her boobs. She was afraid to breathe in too deeply, in case the zipper gave in and burst.

Her hair was a thick mess of curls. She'd briefly considered trying to put it up but quickly shoved that idea aside. It would've taken too long. Her heart raced, beating like mad in her chest. Her mouth felt dry. She had all the classic signs of nerves, including butterflies in her stomach. They were big and flapped like mad. There was a part of her that wanted to turn and walk away but there was a bigger part that needed to know.

Always.

Georgia needed to know what that meant. Was it the

boys? Was that all, or was there more? God, she hoped it meant more. *Please!*

Georgia swallowed thickly as she approached a door where light music was coming from. She could hear people talking. She licked her lips, then admonished herself for taking off her lip gloss. She smoothed her dress, taking in a deep breath – not too big in case her boobs broke loose.

"Hi." She smiled at a guy standing outside the open double doors.

He nodded once at her, retaining his serious expression.

Then she wheeled the stroller into the doorway. There were quite a number of people at the party. Thankfully it wasn't too noisy. The twins should—

Then she spotted him. He was facing sideways. His eyes were locked with that beautiful dragon lady. The one with the long, dark hair and beautiful blue eyes. The one he most definitely had a history with. No doubt about it.

Shale was holding onto her upper arms and he was staring into her eyes with such intensity, she was sure he was going to kiss her. Right there and right then. He didn't though. She found herself pushing out a sigh of relief. Her reprieve didn't last long. The lady smiled at Shale. They seemed to be having a whole conversation with their eyes. One that only people who had been intimate before could have.

His gaze roamed her face, like he was taking her in. The dragon lady brushed her long, hair over her shoulder. It was beautiful and glossy and oh so very straight. She could most likely get that hair into any kind of up-do she wanted. It was the kind of hair that actually listened and did what was expected of it.

She said something to Shale. From the way she said it, it was probably a question. The two of them were so absorbed with one another that Shale hadn't even noticed her standing there.

In fact, he was so busy checking the dragon lady out, that he hadn't even noticed that she'd asked him something. Georgia couldn't blame him. Good god, but that dress she was wearing was amazing. It was really short. Showcasing an amazing pair of legs. No hairs on those babies. *No way!* The dress was tight. So was her body. Her breasts were neat and tidy. Perky as anything. No bra in sight. She didn't need a bra. In fact, she probably didn't even own a bra.

Perky-Tits leaned in a little closer and spoke to Shale again.

"Are you okay?" It was Sand. He had her by the arm and was facing the other way.

Georgia realized that she was panting. Her chest was moving up and down in quick succession. If she didn't get herself under control soon, she was going to have to breathe into a paper bag. "No," she managed to push out. "I'm not."

Georgia couldn't take her eyes off Shale, who finally realized Perky-Tits was talking to him. He wiped the drool off his mouth and gave the goofiest looking smile to dragon lady. The kind of smile a guy got when he had sex on the brain.

Perky-Tits said something else and then pushed those neat little suckers against his chest. His *bare* chest.

Georgia was blinking quickly, trying hard not to cry.

"Come with me," Sand said, returning his gaze to her.

"Let's go," he added, ushering them from the room.

Georgia's lip quivered. She nodded, allowing herself to be led. Sand pushed the stroller. He put an arm around her. "That might not be what you think it is."

"Um… you're a sweet brother, but don't do that…" Georgia shook her head. "We both know exactly what that was." She was shocked at the level of anger in her voice. "I don't know why I'm even reacting like this." She gave another shake of her head, feeling sad all over again. "Shale never promised me anything. In fact, he's always maintained that we're not together. I pushed him to date. I told him to go tonight and to have fun." Her voice broke as she said the word.

Fun!

Hah!

"I guess I never expected—We're going the wrong way," she said. "I'm sure Shale's place is that way." She pointed behind them.

"Here we are." Sand pushed a door open as they turned a corner. He felt along the wall and turned a light on. "My place. I thought you might want some company in a neutral space." They went inside.

It was a bachelor pad to a *T*. Exactly what she had expected to find Shale living in. A pool table dominated the far corner. There was also a foosball table and a wet towel lying on the floor. Sand kicked it to the side, gesturing for her to come in the rest of the way. "I won't bite, you know!"

"Just to be clear." She cocked her head. "Shale might be off… doing whatever he's doing…" she wiped away a tear – stupid, stupid tear, "but I'm not ready to… do anything with you or anyone else. Especially you since you're his twin."

Sand laughed. "I know that. My reasons for flirting with you are two-fold. Firstly, I think you're fucking hot. I mean…" He whistled, giving her the once-over. "Look at you in that dress."

Georgia laughed, despite the tears were still leaking out of her stupid, stupid eyes.

"Secondly, I'm doing it so that my dickhead brother will catch a damn wake up before he loses you. I wish I had gotten to you first, babe, but I can see when I'm beat. You're in love with Shale."

She snorted. "I hardly know Shale, and he's exactly the opposite of my type. He's too good-looking, and a player. He's also arrogant and an ass. I also wish I had met you first. You're really sweet."

Sand choked out a laugh. "Hardly. Let's sit down. I'm going to get you something to drink and then I'm going to call that asshole brother of mine."

"Don't bother." She shook her head. "I doubt he would even answer. He'll be too busy screwing Perky-Tits." She burst into tears. Up until then, she'd had leaky eyes but, in that moment, when saying it out loud, the floodgates opened.

"Oh, angel." Sand opened his arms and she shuffled in closer. She put her head against his chest and balled her eyes out. Like any good friend, he wrapped her up in his arms and hugged her tight. "I'm so sorry," he murmured.

There was a sudden loud crash that frightened the bejesus out of her. "What the fuck is going on here!" Shale snarled.

"It's not what you think." Sand let her go and walked towards Shale. He put up a hand, trying to ward him off.

Shale looked pissed. He looked taller than he normally was. His big muscles now bulged. Especially the ones on either side of his neck... and his biceps. Good lord, but his biceps were huge. Probably because he was clenching his fists.

He growled low, reminding her of an angry tiger. "You fucker!" he roared, all of that animosity aimed at his brother.

There was a crunching noise as his fist met with Sand's jaw. Sand went flying backwards. He used the pool table to keep himself from falling.

"Stop!" she screamed. "Stop it!" she added, when she saw Shale was positioning himself to hit Sand again. *What the hell was he doing? Why was Shale there? Where was the dragon lady?*

"Stop it!" she yelled again as she pushed the stroller as far away from the fighting men as she could get. Then again, Sand was putting up a defensive position. He held his hands up to block any potential blows.

"What are you doing with my female? Mine!" He roared the last.

"Nothing!" Sand yelled. "I swear—"

"Didn't look like fucking nothing." Shale shoved Sand. Thankfully away from where she and the babies were. Sand fell on his ass, landing hard.

"Shale, bro—"

"Don't you dare 'Shale bro' me, you piece of fucking shit." Shale aimed a finger at Sand. "Don't you dare say another word."

Shale turned back to her. His eyes. *Good lord!* They were a bright, glowing golden color and slitted. Shale was a dragon. A fact she still sometimes forgot. He had a couple of scales on his chest as well. They were a beautiful green and iridescent. "Shale," she managed to mutter as she watched him advance.

"We're leaving." His nostrils flared with every deep inhalation. A vein throbbed on his forehead. He took the stroller and began pushing it towards the door.

"It's not—" Sand began.

"Shut the fuck up," Shale said, under his breath, sounding even more terrifying. "Come," he said to her. "Let's go," he added when she didn't move.

"You're scaring me," she said, looking back at Sand. "Are you okay? Will you—"

"Don't talk to him," Shale growled. "Let's go! We need to have a serious conversation and it can't fucking wait."

"You're being an asshole!"

"I'm fine." Sand rubbed his jaw. "Go!"

"You don't get to speak to my female. Not fucking ever!" Shale snarled.

"Don't speak to Sand like that!" She put her hands on her hips. "You can leave. I'm not going anywhere with you."

"Fine!" he grunted, letting the handles of the stroller go. "Stay with him. Hope you guys are very happy together."

"What the hell are you talking about? What's gotten into you? I'm the one who should be angry. Where's your dragon girlfriend?" She blurted the last, wishing she hadn't.

He turned stormy eyes on her. "What dragon girlfri—?" He frowned. "Who, Topaz?" His frown deepened, like he didn't know what she was talking about.

"Topaz," Georgia repeated and then nodded. "Figures

she'd have a name like that," she mumbled. "The one who was rubbing her chest all over you. You had a goofy smile plastered on your face and couldn't stop—"

"I had the goofy look because I was thinking of you and the boys."

"Yeah, right! Like hell! I wasn't born yesterday, you know!"

Sand chuckled from somewhere behind them. He winced and clutched his jaw. "Your female was crying because she saw you and Topaz together looking all cozy. I was consoling her when you busted in."

"Consoling her, my ass," Shale boomed.

"Take a look at your female's eyes, wise-ass. You can see she's been crying, if you actually take the time to look." Sand got up off the ground.

Shale looked at her, his eyes first narrowing and then softening.

"I'm with Georgia on this one. You and Topaz *did* look cozy together." He made a face. "I thought the same as Georgia, for a second. Only, you haven't hung out with Topaz in the longest time. Not Topaz or any other female. I don't think you would start now. Not after the way I've seen you look at Georgia. Not after all this possessive bullshit." He rubbed his jaw again.

"What are you talking about?" she asked Sand.

"It's mating behavior. It's directed at you, Georgie Girl." Sand winked.

Shale growled low and deep.

Sand smirked. "See what I mean? I don't believe for a second that Shale was ever going to take Topaz up on her offer."

She scowled. "I know what I saw," Georgia said. "At

least, that's what it looked like." Maybe she was wrong about the dragon lady. "You *have* slept with her before." God, that came out sounding jealous.

Sand chuckled. "See, you're just as bad as he is."

"I apologize for busting in here and for hitting you without getting the facts first." He turned to her. "I apologize for being a jerk, Georgia. I really think we should go now. We need to talk this through, in private."

Georgia nodded once. "Okay." She looked Sand's way. He was grinning like a madman. "Thank you for your help. Sorry you got beat up."

Sand's grin was gone in an instant. Shale chuckled.

"I didn't get beat up!" Sand half-yelled. "I didn't fight back. There's a big difference."

"Okay, okay." Georgia put up her hands. "Thanks for your help. I'll leave it at that."

"Any time, Georgia." He winked at her.

Shale muttered a curse under his breath. "You're doing that on purpose."

"Damn straight," Sand chuckled.

Shale's lips twitched. "Stop! Your jaw can't take another hit." He pushed the stroller out into the hall. The babies were still sound asleep, which was nuts after all the growling and shouting that had just gone on.

Georgia walked next to them. If she thought her heart had been pounding before, she was wrong. It was pounding *now*. So hard and so loudly that she could barely hear anything else.

CHAPTER 23

They were back at the apartment in what felt like a half a minute but was probably closer to three. The door shut behind them with an ominous click that reverberated around the room.

"I'm going to put the babies in their beds." He pushed the stroller towards their room.

"No." Georgia shook her head. "They're clearly comfortable in their bassinets." She widened her eyes. "They have to be, after sleeping through all that."

He nodded, pushing the stroller so that it was up against the wall.

"So, you..." she began.

"That was..." he said, at the same time. "You go first," Shale said.

"Now that we're here, I don't know what to say." She shook her head. The thing was, she didn't want to make a fool of herself. What if she was still reading this wrong?

"Yes, you do, Georgia. Just say what's on your mind."

She chewed on her lower lip. "Who is Topaz to you?"

"Nothing." He folded his arms. Shale wasn't making this easy for her. He kept his eyes on hers.

"You have… *had* a thing with her?"

Shale shrugged. "Not really. We fucked a couple of times. That's all."

"Oh! Okay." She nodded her head, far too quickly. "I can see why you would… have a thing… with her. I mean, she's really beautiful."

"Yes, she is." His tone softened.

Ouch! It hurt hearing him say it. "You're beautiful in your own way, Georgia. You know that, don't you?"

In her own way. That wasn't really a compliment. Or was it?

He ran a hand through his hair and made a groaning noise that was laced with frustration. "You're overthinking it. All of it. Us! For a fucking gorgeous female, you have zero confidence in yourself. Something I find so goddamn sexy and, at the same time—seriously irritating."

"O-okay," she stammered. *What did you say to that?* He found her sexy and fucking gorgeous. *His* words! Maybe he was saying them because he believed she wanted to hear them. Not because he meant them.

"There you go again." Shale paced away from her a stride or two before walking back. "You were crying earlier. Why?"

"Because… b-because… I thought you were going to leave with her." She licked her lips.

"And?" he pushed.

She shrugged. "I didn't like it."

"Why not, Georgia? Speak to me." He came in closer. "We're not talking to each other here. I've been afraid of bombarding you. Of scaring you away. This…" he gestured around them. "It's all a lot to take in. I felt we could settle into being parents first. Get things straightened out with your mother as well, and then…"

"And then what?"

"According to you, we should move into separate apartments. You want me to start dating other people… yesterday." He widened his eyes. "Yet, when you think I am doing as you asked, you get upset. I'm getting mixed signals here, Mississippi."

She shook her head and swiped a hand over her face, feeling like an idiot. She *had* said that. She had been upset as well.

"What was that about?" he asked.

"I don't want you to move out or to date other people. I said it because I thought it's what you wanted. I don't want to hold you back. You can be a dad to the boys without being *with* me. I don't want you doing anything because you feel obligated. You said it yourself when we first arrived. You said it in front of half your lair. You told everyone that we weren't together. That we were just parents to the twins. That, that was it."

"At the time it was true. Things change, Georgia." He took her hand and squeezed. "I knew then that there was something between us. I wasn't sure if that something was enough. Now I know."

"It's only been a few days." She laughed, but it sounded hollow and a touch nervous.

"It doesn't matter. I know." Shale took her other hand. "I don't want to scare you. I planned on giving you space and it isn't working out so well. I need to tell you my feelings, here." He let her hands go; they felt cold, so she clasped them together. "I can still give you space. I'll even move out, if that's what you want, but I won't be taking Topaz or anyone else up on any offers, and while there's still a chance for us to be together, I might beat anyone who looks at you the wrong way. It might happen often, because you have the finest…" he shook his head. "Let me not be a crass dick right now. I want to explore this." He gestured between them. "Us. Not just because of the babies." He shook his head. "Sand was right. I haven't touched another female since you. I didn't think too much about it. I told myself it was because I was holding out for another human female. I told myself a bunch of bullshit, but I think I felt something… even then. I'm not saying I was pining for you, or that I would have stayed celibate indefinitely, but it was there. A spark. A 'something.'"

"Phew!" She pushed out a breath. "This is a lot to take in. You're right!"

"You're a little nervous, aren't you?"

She nodded. Georgia had been so sure about the two of them. About wanting Shale. Right then though, she was feeling apprehensive, like this was moving too fast all of a sudden. "I told you my dad left when I was little."

He nodded.

"My ex left as well. As soon as things got rough, that was him, gone."

"What happened?" Shale asked, brow furrowing.

"My mom happened. Her illness." Her lip quivered, so she bit down on it for a moment while she pulled herself together. "She was getting worse. The time came to make some tough decisions. Tate wanted me to put her in a state home. One with basic care. I guess she would have been okay, but I couldn't do it. We were saving for our wedding, but I couldn't anymore. Every spare cent I had. Heck! Money I didn't really have, all went to my mom. I also couldn't put her in a home just yet. Not when she still had so many good days. I couldn't do it to her." Her voice hitched. She swallowed down her tears. "I brought her home. To my house with Tate. We had a spare bedroom. I hired nurses. Only part of her care was covered. It meant pushing the wedding out indefinitely, but we could do it. We could still afford our lives and pay for mom." She pushed out a breath.

"What happened?" Shale clenched his jaw. "I can guess."

Georgia nodded. "I struggled with the whole thing. I felt caught between them. My mom and Tate. We fought all the time. It was endless. I felt so much guilt. Guilt because part of me wanted to give in and put her in a home, and guilt for even thinking such a thing. Then I felt guilt because I felt selfish. I was only thinking of my own feelings and not his."

"That's bullshit," Shale growled. "He should never have put you in that position."

"Yes, it was bullshit. When Tate gave me an ultimatum... when he told me to essentially choose between him or my mom..." She shrugged. "It was a no brainer. My mom and I moved out a week later."

"He made you leave?" Shale's eyes had that stormy look again.

"It was his apartment, so yeah, we moved. My mom would never have abandoned me, and I won't ever abandon her."

"We'll go and see her tomorrow."

Georgia felt her heart lift. "Do you mean it?"

Shale nodded.

"That's great." She threw her hands around his shoulders. They both tensed as their bodies touched. Georgia pulled away first.

"So, you need to tell me where we go from here." He tugged on one of her curls. "Mating behavior, New York. That means I'm all in. It didn't take long. Shifters don't need much time, but you're human and you've been hurt. I get that. You know my feelings and we can take things as fast or as slow as you want, but we *communicate* from here on out. You are so used to putting others first. Of assuming what the other person wants and trying to give it to them even if it's to your own detriment. Don't do that anymore, okay?"

She nodded. "I'll try." Her heart raced... with nervous excitement. "I think we should date. Boyfriend and girlfriend."

He smiled, it turned tense when his jaw tightened. "We're exclusive, though."

"Absolutely. I'll get mad if any of those dragon ladies try to rub their perky little breasts on you."

"That's what I'm talking about, Alabama. More of that. Tell me what you want and don't want. Do you want me to move out?"

She shook her head. "We do need to be partners when it comes to those little boys —who we still need to name." She widened her eyes.

"Okay, I'm glad to hear it. What else?"

"We live together but stay in separate rooms... for now."

"I can live with that." He nodded. "This is good. This is great." He nodded. "We're all dressed up so why not have our first date right now. Have you eaten? I can order in?"

"No." She hadn't had a chance.

"I can order us some food and we can set a table and… light some candles and talk. We can talk a whole lot more. There is so much we don't know about one another." He was so incredibly sweet. Shale may have been a player but that was definitely no longer the case.

"Thank you, by the way. Before you say anything more… I have to thank you." She touched the diamond pendants. "For these. They're beautiful." She touched her ears. "For the earrings too. They're also beautiful. Too much!"

"No way! Not nearly enough. You gave me two gorgeous boys."

"Yeah, the labor pains are still fresh in my mind, so I'll keep the set." She widened her eyes. "Even though it's too much."

Shale chuckled but quickly turned serious. "One other thing, Wyoming." He shuffled his feet and then scratched his cheek. "You'll need to let me know how fast or slow… How you feel about… Where you're at with…"

Shale was so cute. So unbelievably adorable right then. "Are you referring to sex, Shale?"

He nodded, suddenly looking more like a little boy than a grown man. This, despite all the muscles and the stubble on his jaw. "I am, yes. I know you just gave birth and that you may not be feeling very… sexy. You might be tired, and you might still have pain or—"

"Shale."

"Yeah?" He raised his brows.

"I'm not all that hungry."

"You're not?" He took a step towards her, his expression growing intense.

"Nope. Not even a little bit." She toyed with the zipper on her dress. Earlier this evening, it had been easy access for the twins. Right then though…

"I am!" His eyes were on her chest. "I'm fucking ravenous right now. Just not for solids." He took a step towards her.

Georgia gasped. Was it sick that hearing him saying that turned her on – and in a bad way?

"Oh yes, Georgia. I think we've reached a point in our conversation where crass is very much allowed." He paused. "Make that, it's encouraged."

"We have?" Her voice sounded husky.

"What I wanted to say earlier was that you have the fucking best pair of tits I've ever seen on a female. They were great before but they're irresistible now. Do it!" He bobbed his brows, his gaze on her hand.

She still had her fingers on the zipper.

"Show me." Holy crap, his pants were tented. His cock jutting from his body.

Georgia felt a little apprehensive. She still wore the feeding bra. Granted, she'd worn it every day. He'd seen her boobs every day since she'd had the boys. This was different. They were being sexy and flirty. How could she be sexy wearing a feeding bra? Not just that, she had those pads in. The ones that absorbed leakage.

"Stop!" Shale growled the word. "Don't even *think* it, Georgia. Look at me. I'm beyond turned on. I want you so fucking badly."

"I'm wearing a feeding bra!" She couldn't help it.

"You don't need silk or lace. Unzip the dress!" His voice was husky, his eyes hooded.

She pulled the zipper down slowly. All the way down to her belly button, and then took the fabric in each hand and pulled it open.

Shale groaned. "Now the bra. It has a front clasp."

"It might get messy. I might leak all—"

"I don't care. I want to see you. All of you. This is how it's going to go down…" She liked it when he was bossy. "You're going to unclasp that bra. I'm going to lift up your dress and tear off whatever underwear you're wearing. I don't care what kind of underwear it is, by the way. You could be wearing granny fucking panties for all I care. I'm still tearing them off and I'm still going to be as turned on as ever. Then, I'm going to get you nice and wet…"

Holy crap. She was wet already. Just hearing him talk had done that. "Once you're dripping, maybe even begging, I'm going to fuck you until you scream my name. It's all going to go down really quickly because I'm afraid of how much time we have and quite frankly I need this. I'm going to assume by your scent right now that you need it too. Then I'm going to let you pick a bedroom… your place or mine," he winked and she giggled, "where I will proceed to make sweet and passionate love to you. I'm going to turn every light on and tell you in infinite detail how fucking sexy you are. If the babies wake up, I'll share you for as long as it takes to get them back to bed and then we're finishing it. You're coming twice. I would promise more, but you also need your rest."

More.

Holy crap.

She had no doubt he could deliver too. "Okay." She unclasped her bra and her heavy breasts sprang free. They literally jumped out of there, like they were being held hostage. Georgia glanced down. Good god, but her nipples were huge. They were tight and pointing at him. "I have to warn you." She sounded apprehensive. "I'm locked and loaded. This could get messy."

She watched his Adam's apple work. His eyes darkened. "I'm counting on it, Michigan." He licked his lips, biting his lower lip between his teeth. "Just one second, hold that messy thought," he spoke as he backtracked and then left the room.

CHAPTER 24

*W*here had he gone?

Had he taken one look at her boobs and done a runner? *Surely not! Of course not!* She needed to pull herself together and to get over her confidence issues.

Shale walked back in, pulling the wrapper off of a box, which he then opened. He looked at the box, his eyes narrowing as he read what it said. "Extra-large. Heavy duty. Ribbed for *her* pleasure."

"Ribbed?" She smiled.

"That's what it says on the box, Kentucky." He grinned. "Don't pretend you're not excited about that little prospect." He winked at her.

Georgia giggled. "As long as it doesn't break this time. You might need to go a little easier."

"Not on your life." He shook his head. A shiver ran down her spine.

"I'm hoping you bought those because you were

hoping to get lucky… with me."

"New box, bought for no one else but you, Alaska."

She choked out a laugh.

Shale advanced on her, his eyes on hers. They were hooded and filled with such lust it took her breath away. He gripped her hips and picked her up, making a growling noise that seemed to emanate from his broad chest. Within a few strides, her ass hit against something. The dining room table.

Shale tossed the condoms on the surface behind her. He leaned down grabbing the hem of her dress and pulled it up. All the way up. The fabric bunched around her hips. She tried not to think about her hairy legs.

He gripped her thighs and lifted her onto the table in one easy movement. His biceps bulged. This man was so gorgeous. He quite literally took her breath away. She wanted to pinch herself. This felt surreal. All of it. Shale looked down as he pulled a leg over his hip.

He'd said he didn't care if she was wearing granny panties. The ones she was wearing were almost as bad as granny underwear. She was wearing a pair of full cotton panties. Not very flattering. Before she could think about it anymore, Shale covered her lips with his in a searing kiss that had her moaning. He cupped her pussy through those cotton undies. Thankfully cotton was absorbent. Georgia mewled as all of her senses went onto high alert. His hand was there, but he wasn't doing anything. If she wasn't anchored on the table, she'd rock into him. Her breathing became ragged. Her eyes were open. His were still closed. His lashes fanning over his cheeks, his tongue still toying with hers. Shale broke the kiss. He put his thumb on her clit and pressed lightly.

Shit.

Holy freaking crap balls it felt good.

She was so achy and needy it was crazy.

"Please tell me you're still *au natural,* Texas. That I get to shove my cock into a big, ginger bush."

Georgia giggled. "That shouldn't sound sexy." She was breathless. It sounded like she'd run a marathon. "It shouldn't turn me on."

There was a tug and a ripping noise as he quite literally ripped her underwear off in a move that had her halfway to orgasm in an instant. That same thumb went back to her clit and he rubbed.

Georgia groaned long and deep. Her eyes closed and her head fell back just a little. When she opened her eyes, he was looking down, biting on his lip again. "I forgot how stunning this pussy was." Shale's jaw tightened as he worked a finger inside her. It slid in easily. In fact, she could hear how wet she was. How completely soaked. His thumb still pressed against her clit, making it throb. Within a few thrusts, he added a second finger to the party, making her mewl in desperation.

He pumped in and out of her in a lazy fashion, his fingers crooked just a touch. Shale rubbed that thumb over her clit softly and slowly. His eyes stayed locked with hers, his face just an inch or two away.

Georgia had been under so much pressure over the last few weeks that she hadn't even touched herself. She couldn't remember when last she'd gotten off. *Forever ago.*

"Shale." Her voice was desperate and deep. Too deep to be hers. "Oh… oh…" Tighter and tighter and tighter… with no release in sight. It felt so good and yet it felt like pure torture. She made these noises, her eyes were wide.

"Oh god... Shale... oh... please..." She was dying.

He slowed even more, his thumb stopped moving and went back to pressing against her instead. His fingers kept going. Slow. Easy. Agonizing. "Do you need to come, Vermont?"

She nodded, groaning. She was panting and mewling and mewling and panting. "So badly."

Shale kept fingering her. He leaned forward. Next thing he was tearing a condom open with his teeth. In... slip... out... slip... in... slip. *Agony.* He kept his finger crooked, it rubbed up on a place inside her that had her wanting to climb the walls. "Shale," she panted.

He made a move with his arm, probably pulling his pants down. That's what it looked like to her. His eyes moved from her pussy to his cock and then back again. "So fucking wet," he ground out. He was so dirty. So damned sexy.

She moaned.

"Nearly there, Connecticut. Nearly..." She could see him doing something. All the while, keeping up the slow, easy thrusting into her.

"There..." He pulled his hand away and she yelled in frustration. Shale hauled her legs around his hips. "You remember from before?"

"Remember what?" Her voice was husky and yet shrill. She was still panting. Her brain not really working so well anymore. Her body vibrated with need.

"The holding. The biting. The hard fucking, Utah...You remember?" He thrust into her. This time she yelled in pure joy at finally being full. At finally having Shale inside her again.

She clutched at his biceps. Her breasts mashed up

against him. Her nipples tingling. She couldn't worry about that now. She didn't care about anything other than coming. "Yes."

"All of it, Florida."

She nodded.

"Hold on tight." His jaw was tight. His eyes dark. He began thrusting. Shale grunted hard with each and every one. He had one hand on the small of her back and the other on her thigh. "You feel good… Fuck!" he growled the last. "Still tight as fuck, Washington."

She wanted to smile, or to say something back, but how could she when she was already so close to coming?

"I have to look at you," Shale groaned. "Need to look." He used his hand, urging her to lie down on the table.

Georgia went with it and lay down. Until her back rested against the hard wood. She put her hands flat on the smooth surface. Her pants, groans and cries filled the room.

Shale's grunts and groans were thankfully just as harsh. He held her thighs, holding them up and open to him. His fingers dug in, but it didn't hurt. All she could feel was that building and coiling. Tighter and tighter. Almost out of control.

Her boobs shook and jerked with every hard thrust. "Like a smorgasbord. A fucking buffet." His eyes roamed her body. His grunts were harsh. Every muscle bulged. His abs popped. "Fuck! Arizona. Shit! Michigan. Carolina, Utah, Louisiana, Wyoming. Fuuuuuck… Nebraska." His balls hit up against her ass with every state. "Kansas, Montana." Each word was a little more desperate sounding. *Good!* She was feeling just as desperate. Just as out of control. "Maryland… fuckshitfuuuuck…"

He lifted her ass a little off the table and crouched over her. "Georgia." He forced her name out as his body began to jerk into her. "Geor…" She didn't get to hear the rest of it. She came so long and so hard she was sure she broke something.

By the noises Shale made, maybe it was him she had broken. It took a while for him to slow in his movements. For him to slump over her. He was breathing heavily. But then again, so was she.

That's when she realized how much her breasts were tingling. There was warmth. Plenty of warmth as milk leaked from her nipples. "Oh no! Oh… Shale…"

"I know… they've been doing that for half a minute already. There was a bit of a squirt when you orgasmed."

"No, there—!"

He wiped at his chest which—Georgia groaned and put a hand over her face. There were droplets of something on his chest. *No, surely… Arghhhh!*

"No need to get like that about the whole thing. I thought it was sexy as fuck. Why do you think I had to start naming all the states? It was that or come early. I almost messed that whole thing up, and all because you're so damned sexy. Who knew leaky mom boobs were just as good as sex toys? Make that better." He planted a kiss on the side of her mouth.

"You can't be serious."

"I mean it, Illinois." Shale winked. "You might need to breastfeed those kids until they're six… or seven."

She pushed out a laugh.

Shale pulled out, looking down. He heaved a sigh of relief. "All in one piece." Then he put up a hand. "Not that I would mind a whole house full of kids but," he laughed when he caught her look of horror, "but, we'll wait until One and Two are a little older before we start trying again."

"I should hope so."

"Let me take care of this and I'll bring you a towel. We—"

It was like the little bundles of joy heard their names—*'Please don't let One and Two stick,'* she thought—because they began to wail. Both of them. Together.

Shale smiled.

She did too.

"It looks like they might be getting into that routine after all," she remarked.

"Looks like it. I'll get them. You feed, I'll set up the diaper station." He spoke quickly. It was so cute. "Because I really want to get back to it."

"Me too."

"Okay, then!" He almost jogged to the nursery. She pulled down her dress and went to sit on the sofa. Georgia propped up the pillows while Shale fetched the little ones. She still marveled at how well he handled them both together. *Easy peasy.*

He handed them to her, watching as each baby latched. "Not too much now, boys." Shale winked at her. "Save some for daddy."

She laughed.

CHAPTER 25

The next day...

"I thought we were going to the balcony." Georgia frowned. "Isn't Storm meeting us there?" *What was going on?* Maybe they were headed for another balcony. The helicopter was supposed to be fully fueled and ready for take-off.

Shale put a hand to the small of her back. He had a strange smile in his face. "I told you we were going to see your mom, and I meant it." He opened the door and gestured for her to go in.

Georgia walked through the threshold fully expecting to see a chopper. Instead, she stopped in her tracks. Her mouth fell open and she made a gasping noise, stepping back. She covered her mouth with her hand. "Jennifer? What are you doing here?" she all but whispered. "Mom!" she mouthed.

Jennifer beamed. She put a finger over her lips, looking down at Georgia's mother.

Her mom was sitting on a single couch. She had a blanket over her lap and was gazing out at the beautiful view. She seemed serene. Completely content. Georgia looked around the room. It was big and airy. There was a bed like the one at the home; it had sides that could be clipped up, so that her mom couldn't fall out at night.

The plugs were covered, and the cupboard doors had been sealed with child-proof locks. She somehow knew that if she checked the bathroom, there would be a handrail next to the toilet and another one in the shower. This place had been transformed.

Her mom laughed. She actually laughed. Her eyes were wide and filled with delight. Georgia followed her line of sight, spotting a dragon flying by. Her mother laughed again, this time clapping her hands. Georgia found herself smiling too. Then the tears came. Her mom was here. Not only that, she looked happy.

"She does that every time a shifter flies past." Jennifer lowered her voice even further. "I still can't believe it. I'm in awe myself." She smiled broadly.

Shale wheeled the stroller in. He was smiling too. "I'm sorry I didn't tell you about this. I wanted it to be a surprise." Shale put an arm around her and pulled her in close. "I must say, I thought you'd be happier."

"I am," she sobbed out the words. "Happier than I ever believed possible." She buried her face in his chest. "Thank you so much. This is more than I ever imagined—" she whispered.

"We're a family," Shale whispered back "I know I'm

moving too quickly here. You don't have to say anything back, but I need you to know that we belong together. That means your mom as well."

She threw her arms around his neck and hugged him close. Still crying. There was no way she could stop the waterworks. Her heart felt like it was going to burst out of her chest with emotion.

Something vibrated between them, making her give a little squeal. Georgia stepped back.

"My phone." He shrugged. "It can wait," he added, taking her hand. "For now, we only have one nurse to take care of your mom. I will hire more staff. You will need to assist with it. If you don't mind."

"Of course, yes. I…"

His phone began to vibrate again. "What could be so important?" Shale said.

"You'd better answer it."

Shale's jaw was tight. He swiped the screen and said, "Hello. Yes…" He frowned as he listened to the person on the other side. "Are you sure?" He listened intently to whatever it was that they were saying. "What are you getting at?" Shale muttered a curse. "I hope he hasn't done something stupid." He listened again for a beat or two, then barked. "Keep me informed." He swiped the screen again, looking deep in thought and very worried.

"What is it?"

"I'm not sure." Shale shook his head. His whole body vibrated with energy. "It might be nothing."

"What happened?" Something had happened. That much was apparent.

"Your friend, Macy, and my brother, Sand went back

to your place to pick up some of your things."

"Macy?" It was Georgia's turn to frown.

"She was at your mother's facility when the males arrived there earlier. A team came back here with your mom. Two of the males stayed behind to pick up some of your things. You made a list."

Georgia nodded. "I had told Macy I was visiting my mom today. That's why she was at the care facility. I hope you don't mind?"

"No. That's fine." Shale nodded once. "They went through to your place to fetch some of your things and that's where it gets complicated."

"How so?" Georgia swallowed thickly.

"They disappeared."

"Who did?" Georgia looked perplexed. "You're not making sense here."

"Sand and Macy. One minute they were there and the next they were gone."

"Like magic?"

Shale chuckled but quickly sobered. "Not quite, Michigan." He took to frowning and looking very worried all over again. "The male who was with them went to check on a noise he heard outside. Sand stayed inside with Macy. When the male returned a minute later, they were gone. No signs of a struggle. He didn't hear anything out of the ordinary. He didn't see anything out of place." Shale looked contemplative. "Do you think that your friend would…" he shrugged, "hook-up with Sand?"

"Do you think they… that they," she widened her eyes, "you know… decided to get some quiet time together?"

"I wouldn't put it past Sand. He's a horny bastard

but…" Shale shook his head. "I'm concerned because he normally takes his duties really seriously. It's not like him to just fuck around like that. Yet, at the same time, I wouldn't put it past him either."

"Macy did spend the night with Rock but," Georgia shook her head. "it wasn't normal behavior for her. She's more of a relationship type. I can't see her making a habit of it, but," she shrugged, "who knows? Do you think they left to go and… have sex?" she whispered.

Shale chuckled softly. "People have sex all the time. It isn't such a big deal. Only, Sand should know better and usually does." He got a little animated. "He'll be in big shit when he comes back."

"You still look really worried," Georgia said. "I can see you're making light of this, but you're not completely buying it."

"I'm hoping he *has* gone off to have sex with your friend because the other option is too worrying to contemplate."

"What is it? What else could have happened?"

"The hunters got them. That is my concern. Word got out about our boys. About their chest markings. Hunters may have come in and… staked your place out. They saw an opportunity and got to them."

"Yeah but, without a sound? How is that even possible?"

"That's just it – and it gives me hope they're just fooling around. We'll know for sure in a day or two, at most. If they're gone for longer, we know it's something more sinister." He put his arms around her and squeezed. "I'm sure it's just Sand being Sand. I know you haven't noticed, but he's a charmer."

She giggled. "I hadn't noticed at all. I'm sure they'll turn up really soon." Anxiety churned inside her though.

A couple of weeks later...

Shale came back inside, worry clouded his eyes. He forced a smile as soon as he saw her. "Did you get the boys down okay?"

"Yes." She smiled. "They're fast asleep for their afternoon nap, like clockwork. I take it that there is still no news?"

Shale shook his head. "Three private investigators on the case and still nothing. It's like they vanished into thin air."

Worry churned in her gut for both Sand and Macy. "I wonder where they could have gotten to."

Shale shook his head. "The hunters have them. There's no other explanation."

She nodded. "Do you think they're still alive?" She bit down on her lip, trying to hold back the emotion that welled up.

Shale nodded, he squeezed the back of his neck and pushed out a heavy breath. "I hope so, Georgia. I really hope so." His jaw tightened for a few moments. "My brother is worth too much alive."

"And Macy?" Her voice was shrill.

"Sand wouldn't let anything happen to her, but he can be rash. Shit! I wish I knew where they were so that I could help them."

"I know. Me too." Her eyes filled with tears.

"Don't cry, Texas." Shale hooked an arm around her waist. "Please sweetheart, you know it kills me when you cry. I can't take it." He placed a kiss on the side of her mouth.

"I know, I just… I worry." She sniffed, blinking hard.

"Yeah, Sand will die to protect Macy and they need him so… I'm sure they'll be okay. He's tougher than he looks." Shale smiled, it reached his eyes. His features softened despite their conversation. "On a lighter note, I have news that I think will help you feel at least marginally better."

"What news is that?"

His smiled grew bigger. "The Joyces' adoption of a little girl went through this morning. She was born a couple of days ago."

"What?" she half yelled, quickly putting a hand over her mouth and listening for a wail. When no sound came from the monitor, she went on. "How do you know?"

Shale shrugged. "I've stayed in touch."

She narrowed her eyes. "Stayed in touch, my ass."

"Okay, I may have put in a good word with the adoption agency and with the birth mother of the child. She's only sixteen. She was on the street."

"Was?" Georgia raised her brows.

Shale shrugged again. "She has a place to live now and she'll get an education. She's a good kid who was down on her luck."

"You're amazing, you know that?" Georgia's heart swelled. Her eyes filled with tears all over again. This time they were good ones.

"Yeah… well." He gave a rueful grin.

"No, I mean it. You're a good guy, Shale. One of the best… and I love you so much." It still felt weird saying it, since they'd only just started doing it. It felt good though too. It felt right.

"Anything to make you happy, Wyoming." He winked and she giggled. "When are you moving in with me? This whole 'your room or mine' thing is getting old fast."

"After we're mated." She bobbed her brows.

"Three more weeks and then you're in my arms every night from dusk till dawn? I can't wait." His voice became animated.

She laughed. "We sleep together every night now already. It's just a stupid formality."

"One I can't—"

There was an almighty crash. Glass splintered... noise and chaos erupted. Shale spun to her, shielding her with his body. She would have been thrown off her feet if it weren't for his strong arms banding around her.

It went from chaos to calm in an instant. "You okay?" Shale's expression was concerned. He cupped her chin in his big hand.

"Y-yes." she managed to mutter.

"You're not hurt?" he growled.

She shook her head. They both turned to what had caused the ruckus. A dragon lay in a heap on their living room floor. One of the sofas was on its side. Their coffee table was no longer. It was a splintered mess under the dragon. "What in the—?" she began.

"Sand!" Shale boomed.

The dragon lifted his great head. Its eyes were filled with confusion for a moment. Then they rolled back in its skull, his head crashed back down.

"By claw!" Shale yelled, running over to the downed creature. "Sand!" He shouted.

Georgia watched as the dragon folded in on itself, until a man lay on the ground. He was panting heavily and groaned every so often.

She walked over to them. "I can't believe it," she whispered. "It's him!"

Shale continued to try to rouse his twin. "Sand." He rubbed his back and shook him. "Brother, please!"

Sand finally lifted his head again, still panting. His eyes were hazy, as if he was drunk or something.

"He's exhausted," Shale explained. "Where were you?" he tried again.

"Macy," Sand muttered. "Mace…" he said again.

"Where is she?" Georgia yelled, crouching next to Sand. "What happened to you?" She looked over at Shale. "What can I do to help him?"

"Need a team of males… need to go back…" He pulled himself up, looking stronger.

One of the babies cried over the monitor. "That's Gossan," she muttered absently. He had become the lighter sleeper of the two. Then again, she could hardly expect him to could sleep through the commotion of a dragon crashing through their house. "I'll go…" she began.

Sand gave a groggy smile. "Gossan, after father." He shook his head "The old man must be thrilled."

"He is quite. You still haven't—"

"And my other nephew?" Sand asked, just as both boys began yelling over the monitor.

"Granite," Georgia said. "We named him after your brother. He stuck his neck out and gave permission for my mom…"

"What?" Sand scowled. "I thought I was your favorite,

Georgie. I'm hurt."

"Stop with the bullshit!" Shale growled. "You should lay back down. I'm calling for a healer."

"No." Sand shook his head vehemently. "Assemble a team of males. We need to go and rescue Macy. She is safe, but not for very long."

"Those hunters!" Shale snarled. "We can't just head off to god knows where, to—"

"It's not the hunters who have her." Sand shook his head, a deep frown marring his forehead.

Then the babies began screaming in earnest, drowning out whatever it was that Sand was saying. Georgia got up to go to them, her heart pounding.

The
END

AUTHOR'S NOTE

Charlene Hartnady is a USA Today Bestselling author. She loves to write about all things paranormal including vampires, elves and shifters of all kinds. Charlene lives on an acre in the country with her husband and three sons. They have an array of pets including a couple of horses.

She is lucky enough to be able to write full time, so most days you can find her at her computer writing up a storm. Charlene believes that it is the small things that truly matter like that feeling you get when you start a new book, or when you look at a particularly beautiful sunset.

BOOKS BY THIS AUTHOR

The Chosen Series:

Book 1 ~ Chosen by the Vampire Kings
Book 2 ~ Stolen by the Alpha Wolf
Book 3 ~ Unlikely Mates
Book 4 ~ Awakened by the Vampire Prince
Book 5 ~ Mated to the Vampire Kings (Short Novel)
Book 6 ~ Wolf Whisperer (Novella)
Book 7 ~ Wanted by the Elven King

Shifter Night Series:

Book 1 ~ Untethered
Book 2 ~ Unbound
Book 3 ~ Unchained
Shifter Night Box Set Books 1 - 3

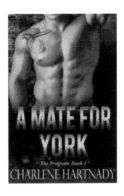

The Program Series (Vampire Novels)
Book 1 ~ A Mate for York
Book 2 ~ A Mate for Gideon
Book 3 ~ A Mate for Lazarus
Book 4 ~ A Mate for Griffin
Book 5 ~ A Mate for Lance
Book 6 ~ A Mate for Kai
Book 7 ~ A Mate for Titan

The Feral Series
Book 1 ~ Hunger Awakened
Book 2 ~ Power Awakened

Demon Chaser Series (No cliffhangers)
Book 1 ~ Omega
Book 2 ~ Alpha
Book 3 ~ Hybrid
Book 4 ~ Skin
Demon Chaser Boxed Set Book 1–3

The Bride Hunt Series (Dragon Shifter Novels)
Book 1 ~ Royal Dragon
Book 2 ~ Water Dragon
Book 3 ~ Dragon King
Book 4 ~ Lightning Dragon
Book 5 ~ Forbidden Dragon
Book 6 ~ Dragon Prince

The Water Dragon Series
Book 1 ~ Dragon Hunt
Book 2 ~ Captured Dragons
Book 3 ~ Blood Dragon
Book 4 ~ Dragon Betrayal

The Earth Dragon Series
Book 1 ~ Dragon Guard
Book 2 ~ Savage Dragon
Book 3 ~ Dragon Whelps

Dragon HUNT

WATER DRAGONS BOOK 1

CHARLENE HARTNADY

CHAPTER 1

S he should be happy.

What was she thinking? She *was* happy.

Happy, excited and nervous all rolled into one. Nervous? Hah! She was quaking in her heels. This was a huge risk. Especially now. Her stomach clenched and for a second she wanted to turn around and head back into her boss's office. Tell him she'd changed her mind.

No.

She would regret it if she didn't take this opportunity. Why now though? Why had this fallen into her lap now? What if it didn't work out? She squeezed her eyes closed as her stomach lurched again.

"You okay?" Rob's PA asked, eyebrows raised.

Jolene realized she was standing outside her boss's office, practically mid-step. Hovering.

"Fine." She pushed out the word together with a pent-up breath. She *was* fine, she realized. More than fine, and she had this. The decision was already made. Her leave approved. She was doing this, dammit. Jolene smiled. "I'm great."

"Good." Amy smiled back. "Just so you know," she said under her breath, looking around them to check that no-one was in hearing distance, "I'm rooting for you." She winked.

"Thank you. I appreciate that," Jolene said as she headed back to her office, trying not to think about it. Not right now. It would make her doubt her decision all over again. She'd made the right one. The only thing holding her back was fear of failure. It was justifiable and yet stupid. She wasn't going to live with regrets because fear held her back. She was going to embrace this. Give it her all and then some. Her step suddenly felt lighter as she walked into her office. *Do not look left.* Whoever designed this building had been a fruitcake. This floor was large and open-plan. Fifty-three cubicles. There were only two offices. One was hers, and one was—*Not looking or thinking about her right now.* Both offices had glass instead of walls. Why bother? Why even give her an office in the first place if everyone could see into it?

It had something to do with bringing management closer to their staff, or the other way round – she couldn't remember. The Execs were on the next floor. *Not going there and definitely not looking left.* She could feel a prickling sensation on that side of her body. Like she was being watched. Jolene sat down at her desk and opened her laptop. Her accepted leave form was already in her inbox. She had to work hard not to smile. It was better to stay impassive. Especially when anyone could look in on her. This was going to work out. It would. All of it.

No more blind dates.

No more Tinder.

No more friends setting her up.

She was done! Not only was she done with trying to find a partner, she was done with human men in general. Jolene bit down on her bottom lip, thinking of the letter inside her purse. She'd been accepted.

Yes!

Whooo hooo!

It was all sinking in. She couldn't quite comprehend that this was actually happening.

The sound of her door opening snapped her attention back to the present. She lifted her head from her computer screen in time to see Carla saunter in. No knock. No apologies for interrupting. Not that Jolene had been doing anything much right then, but still. She could have been.

A smug smile greeted her. "I believe I'm filling in for you starting Friday for three weeks." Her colleague and biggest adversary sat down without waiting for an invitation. "Rob just called to fill me in."

"Yes," she cleared her throat, "that's right." Jolene nodded. *Don't let her get to you.* "I have too many leave days outstanding and decided to take them."

Carla folded her arms and leaned back. She seemed to be scrutinizing Jolene. It made her uncomfortable. "Yeah, but right now? You're either really sure of yourself or…"

She let the sentence drop. "I believe you're going on a singles' cruise?" The smirk was back. Carla's beady eyes—not really, they were wide and blue and beautiful—were glinting with humor and very much at Jolene's expense.

It was her own fault. She should never have told Rob about why she was taking this trip. Why the hell had he told Carla? It was none of her damned business. *Stay cool!* She smiled, folding her arms. "I thought it would be fun."

"You do know that I'm about to close the Steiner deal, right? Work on the Worth's Candy campaign is coming along nicely as well."

"Why are you telling me this?" Her voice had a definite edge which couldn't be helped. Carla irritated the crap out of her.

The other woman shrugged. "It might not be the best time for you to go on vacation. Not that I'm complaining. It works for me." Another shrug, one-shouldered this time.

Jolene pulled in a breath. "I need a break. That's the long and short of it."

"Yeah, but right now and on a singles' cruise… do you really think you'll meet someone?" She scrunched up her nose.

"Why not? It's perfectly plausible that I would meet someone. Someone really great!" she blurted, wanting to kick herself for the emotional outburst.

"It's not like you have the greatest track record." Carla widened her eyes. Unfortunately, working in such close proximity for years meant that Carla knew a lot about her. In the early days, they had even been friends.

"But you should definitely go," Carla went on. "You shouldn't let that stop you," she quickly added. Her comments biting.

"I'm not going to let anything stop me. Not in any aspect of my life," Jolene replied, thrilled to hear her voice remained steady.

Carla stood up, smoothing her pencil skirt. "I'll take care of things back here. The reason I popped in was to request a handover meeting, although I'm very much up to speed with everything that goes on around here." She gestured behind her. "I'll email a formal request anyway." She winked at Jolene.

Jolene had to stop herself from rolling her eyes. "Perfect." She refolded her arms, looking up at Carla who was still smiling angelically.

"I need you to know that I plan on taking full advantage of your absence."

"I know." Jolene smiled back. "I'm not worried."

The smile faltered for a half a second before coming back in full force. "You enjoy your trip. Good luck meeting someone." She laughed as she left. It was soft and sweet and yet grating all at once. Like the idea of Jolene actually meeting someone was absurd.

That woman.

That bitch!

Stay impassive. Do not show weakness. Do not show any kind of emotion. She forced herself to look down at her screen, to scroll through her emails.

Two minutes later, there was a knock at her door. Jolene looked up, releasing a breath when she saw who it was. Ruth smiled holding up two cups of steaming coffee.

Jolene smiled back and gestured for her to come in.

"I was in here Xeroxing—our printer is down yet again

– and thought you could use a cup of joe." Ruth ran the admin department on the lower level. Her friend moved her eyeballs to the office next door to hers. The one where Carla sat, separated by just a glass panel.

"You were right," Jolene exclaimed.

Ruth sat down. "Are you okay? That whole exchange looked a little rough."

"I thought I kept my cool. Are you saying you could see how badly she got to me?" Carla was all about pushing buttons. She only won if Jolene retaliated and she'd learned a long time ago it wasn't worth doing so.

"You looked fine. What gave it away and – only because I know you so well – was the way you tapped your fingers against the side of your arm every so often. I take it when 'you know who' said something mean." Ruth handed her the coffee and took a seat.

"Mean doesn't begin to cut it. Thanks for this." She held up the mug before taking a sip.

"What's going on?"

"Things have happened so quickly, I didn't get a chance to tell you. I'm going on vacation." Jolene briefly told her friend all about her real upcoming plans, as well as about what had transpired between Carla and her.

Ruth smiled. "I can't believe you're this excited." She looked at her like she had lost all her faculties. "It's not that big of a deal. Quite frankly, I'm inclined to partly agree with Carla, for once." She made a face. "Maybe you shouldn't be going on a trip right now."

"It's a huge deal, and you're right, I'm excited," Jolene gushed. "One in five hundred applicants are accepted, and I'm one of them. The shifter program is just the place for a woman like me. I'm ready to settle down, to get married and to have kids. Lots of kids. Four or five... okay, maybe five's too many, but four has a ring to it. Two boys and two girls."

"Two of each." Ruth chuckled under her breath.

She smiled as well and shook her head. "Actually, I'm not too fazed about that. I just can't believe they actually selected me."

"You're nuts!" Ruth laughed some more. "Why's it so hard to believe? Just because you've had a bad run doesn't mean you're not... worthy."

"I'm thirty-four. I turn thirty-five in two months' time."

"And that's a big deal why?"

"Because thirty-five is the cut-off for taking part in the program." She had to undergo a whole lot of testing – including ones of the medical variety – and she'd been selected anyway. "I'm so done with guys running away as soon as they realize I'm serious."

"How is being a part of this program going to change anything? I love you long freaking time, but you do tend to scare men away. You're a little... pushy."

"I'm not pushy! I know what I want and I go after it. After everything I've been through, I'm not interested in anything less, and shifters actually want to settle down. They want kids. They want what I want. For once, I'm going to meet someone who doesn't run scared at the prospect of commitment and family." She sucked in a deep breath.

"Human guys also want commitment." Ruth raised her brows, taking another sip of her coffee. "They want kids."

"Just not with me they don't. None of them wanted anything other than sex or casual dating. Sure, they're more than willing to take the plunge as soon as they move on to the next one, but not with me."

"Have you ever stopped to consider that you're maybe coming on just a little too strong? You can't start out a relationship talking about marriage. Guys can't handle that."

"I'm not coming on too strong. I'm done wasting my time… that's all." Jolene took a sip of her own coffee, feeling the warm liquid slide down her throat. "I know what I want. Casual sex, endless dating…" She shook her head. "That's not it. Even living together. Have you ever heard the saying, 'why buy the cow if you can get the milk for free'? No… not for me. Never again!"

"You seem to think it's going to be different with a shifter. Can't say I know too much about shifters." Ruth shrugged. "Except that they're ultimately guys too."

"For starters they're hot. Muscular, tall and really, really good-looking."

"Okay, that's a good start." Ruth leaned forward, eyes on Jolene.

"They have a shortage of their own women, just like with the vampires. It's actually the vampires who are helping them set up this whole dating program."

"Oh!" Ruth looked really interested at this point. "No women of their own you say, now that's interesting."

"I didn't say no women, just not many women. Their kind stopped having female children, so there's a shortage. They have a natural drive to mate and procreate, which is exactly what I'm looking for." Jolene put her coffee down and rubbed her hands together. "I can't wait to get my hands on one."

"You might just be onto something here. Where do I sign up?" her friend whisper-yelled while smiling broadly.

"I can't believe you told Rob you're going on a cruise. Where did you come up with that?"

"I shouldn't have said anything at all." She shook her head. "I don't know why I disclosed as much as I did."

"Yeah!" Ruth raised her brows. "I can't believe he told," she looked to the side while keeping her head facing forwards, "her."

"I know. Thing is, I've made up my mind. I'm going."

"That cow is going to move in while you're gone. She might just get the edge in your absence and take the promotion out from under you."

"I realize that, and yet I can't miss out on this opportunity. I'm willing to risk my career over this. It's a no-brainer for me." She sighed. "Don't get me wrong, I'm freaking out about it, but as much as I love my job, having a family would trump everything. I have a good feeling about this."

"Those shifters sound so amazing." Ruth bobbed her brows.

"I'll show you the website online. They only take three groups a year and then only six women are chosen each time. Just a handful from thousands of applications." Jolene's heartbeat all the faster for getting accepted. She was so lucky! Things had to work out for her. They just had to.

"You say these shifters are hot and pretty desperate?" Ruth smiled, her eyes glinting. "Why didn't you tell me about this sooner? We should have entered together."

"Not exactly desperate, but certainly looking for love. Ninety-six percent of the women who sign up end up mated... that's what the shifters call it, mated. It's not actually the same as marriage, it's more binding. Ninety-six percent," she shook her head, "I rate those odds big time."

"I can't believe you didn't tell me sooner." Even though she was still smiling, Ruth narrowed her eyes. "I thought we were friends."

Jolene made a face. "I didn't tell you anything because I didn't want to jinx it."

Ruth rolled her eyes. "I wouldn't get too excited until you get there. Until you actually meet them." Ruth snickered. "With your luck, you'll get one of the bad apples."

"You shut your mouth. Don't be putting such things out in the universe."

Ruth looked at her with concern. "I don't want you getting your hopes up, that's all."

"Well too late, my hopes are already up." Jolene was going to win herself a shifter. Someone sweet and kind and loving. A man she could spend forever with. "I just wish it wasn't right now. This isn't a good time to be leaving."

"Not with that big promotion on the horizon." Ruth shook her head. "Not when *she* could take it."

"We're both on the same level. We both started at the same time. I hate how evenly matched we are."

"You're the better candidate though. I've never known anyone to work as hard as you."

"Carla works hard too. She's also brought in several big clients in the last couple of months, and she's not going on vacation. She'll be here day in and day out, whispering sweet nothings into Rob's ear."

Ruth made a face. "It's not like that, is it?"

"No, no." She waved a hand. "Sweet nothings of the

business kind. It's still a threat just the same to me, and honestly, that's the only downside to this. I stand a good chance of losing to Carla if I go."

"But you are still going anyway." Ruth took a sip of her coffee, frown lines appearing on her forehead.

"I have to." She pushed out a breath. Hopefully, Ruth was wrong about the whole 'bad apple' thing.

Out now!

Printed in Great Britain
by Amazon